"Sloan, I have to talk to you!"

As soon as she entered the parlor, Carter stepped out of the shadows and pinned her against the wall with his body.

"Sloan, Sloan," he groaned into her hair, nuzzling it with his mouth and nose.

"No, Carter." The firelight had just enough life remaining to dance on his hair, burnishing the deep russet strands to copper. She longed to plow through the mass and hold his head fast against her neck where his face had burrowed.

She forfeited her chance. His head came up suddenly, fiercely, and it was his fingers that threaded through her hair, holding her head still as he stared into the swirling pools of her eyes.

"I've been a good little boy all day. I haven't done one thing to be ashamed of. I've sat at that typewriter all afternoon trying to come up with a sentence that has a subject and a verb and makes some kind of sense, and I'll be damned if I could. I've not had one idea that didn't involve you. I've thought of nothing but you since you opened that door last night—"

WHAT ARE *LOVESWEPT* ROMANCES?

They are stories of true romance and touching emotion. We believe those two very important ingredients are constants in our highly sensual and very believable stories in the *LOVESWEPT* line. Our goal is to give you, the reader, stories of consistently high quality that may sometimes make you laugh, sometimes make you cry, but are always fresh and creative and contain many delightful surprises within their pages.

Most romance fans read an enormous number of books. Those they truly love, they keep. Others may be traded with friends and soon forgotten. We hope that each *LOVESWEPT* romance will be a treasure—a "keeper." We will always try to publish

LOVE STORIES YOU'LL NEVER FORGET
BY AUTHORS YOU'LL ALWAYS REMEMBER

The Editors

LOVESWEPT • 22

Sandra Brown
Breakfast In Bed

 BANTAM BOOKS • TORONTO • NEW YORK • LONDON • SYDNEY

BREAKFAST IN BED

A Bantam Book / November 1983

LOVESWEPT and the wave device are trademarks of Bantam Books, Inc.

ISBN 0-553-21623-6

Published simultaneously in the United States and Canada

Bantam Books are published by Bantam Books, Inc. Its trademark, consisting of the words "Bantam Books" and the portrayal of a rooster, is Registered in U.S. Patent and Trademark Office and in other countries. Marca Registrada. Bantam Books, Inc., 666 Fifth Avenue, New York, New York 10103.

PRINTED IN THE UNITED STATES OF AMERICA

O   0 9 8 7 6 5 4 3 2 1

Chapter One

The moment she saw him, she knew it had been a mistake to grant Alicia's favor.

There he stood on the porch of Fairchild House with his suitcase in one hand, his portable typewriter in the other, his narrow-framed tortoise shell eyeglasses on top of his head, looking a trifle sheepish for obviously having gotten her out of bed.

And there she was, Sloan Fairchild, owner and proprietor of the bed and breakfast establishment, standing just inside the arched front door, clutching her robe to her throat with white-knuckled fingers and shifting from one bare foot to the other.

With her first look into Carter Madison's face, her stomach lurched, tightened, then stumbled over itself on its rolling descent to the cushiony floor of her torso. She became acutely aware of her nakedness beneath her nightgown and robe. Between her thighs an unspeakably shameful, yet magnificent, tingling was reminding her of her sex.

"Sloan? Ms. Fairchild?" he asked.

Her head bobbed up and down stupidly.

"Carter Madison. I got you out of bed, didn't I?"

Her tousled hair, her attire, and her bare feet, which he had smiled at, were dead giveaways. "Yes. I'm sorry for—" Her hand began a sweeping gesture down her body, thought better of it, and clutched again at the collar of her robe. "I . . . I thought you'd arrive earlier in the day. Come in."

She moved aside, opening the thick oak door wider. He dragged himself and the cases he carried through the passage. "I'd planned to fly up earlier in the day, but David had a soccer game and he pitched a billy fit when he found out I was going to miss it. I called and changed my flight. The game was scheduled for after school, so by the time it was over and we had celebrated the victory with hamburgers and shakes, I barely made it to the airport in time for the last flight. Didn't Alicia call you?"

"No."

"I'm sorry," he sighed. "She was supposed to call and tell you I'd be late." He set his cases on the floor and flexed his shoulders.

"It doesn't matter. Really."

He straightened to his full height and looked down at her. Eyes, so unusual she'd never seen the like before, collided with hers. Even the faint glow shed by the night lights she kept on in the hallways reflected their light brown, sherry color. They were outlined by thick lashes the same rich, mahogany color of his hair that was streaked with burnished highlights.

"I hate to have inconvenienced you by getting you out of bed. Alicia said you were reluctant to have me staying here in the first place." His lop-sided grin was a little too self-confident, a little too cocky, and absolutely captivating.

Sloan self-consciously pushed back a wayward strand of hair and willed that unprecedented disturbance in the lower part of her body to go away. "Not you specifically, Mr. Madison," she replied in a voice she hoped sounded crisply efficient. "Most bed and breakfast houses are managed by a couple. Since I'm a single woman, I've restricted my guests to only couples or women traveling together."

His eyes slid down her body assessingly. "That might not be a bad idea. You have Fairchild House's reputation to think of."

"Exactly," she said, drawing the robe even tighter around her. The tour his eyes had taken hadn't gone unnoticed by her body, over which she suddenly seemed to have no control. Here she had lived comfortably with it for nearly thirty years, and now in the last two minutes it had gone haywire and become a stranger to her.

"You don't think that policy will cost you business?"

She had the grace to smile. "I'm barely breaking even. I need every paying guest I can get."

"I'm a paying guest," he said. Somehow the soft affirmation sounded like an intimate prophecy.

She pulled herself up to a military posture. "I agreed to let you stay here only because you're my best friend's fiancé and she asked me to house you for a month so you could write the last chapter of your novel before the wedding."

"*Sleeping Mistress.*"

"Pardon?"

"*Sleeping Mistress.* That's the title of the book."

"Oh."

"Have you read my books?"

"Yes."

"Did you like them?"

"Parts of them. I—"

"Which parts?"

"Most parts," she said, laughing at his probing curiosity. Her answer pleased him, but his smile became a little too warm, a little too personal for her already reeling senses. "I think it's wonderful about you and Alicia," she interjected quickly.

"She's a terrific lady."

"Yes she is. I thought . . . never mind."

"Go on. You thought what?"

"Well I thought she'd never recover after Jim got killed. She and the boys took his death so hard. When I talked to her the other day, she sounded very happy. You're responsible. I know you handled most of the legal ramifications for her after his death."

"I was in China at the time of the accident. As soon as I could, I came home. Jim Russell had been my best friend for years. It wasn't a chore, but an honor to look after his widow for him."

To the point of marrying her? Sloan wanted to ask. This time she kept silent. She'd made the mistake of broaching the subject with Alicia.

"This marriage means so much to me, Sloan," Alicia had said. "Ever since Jim . . . well, you know how lonely I've been and what a handful the boys are for me. Carter's been terrific, patient with them and me, but he's about at the end of his rope, too. I think we need a break from each other before we take that final plunge."

"Alicia," Sloan had said hesitantly, "do you love Carter?"

There was a noticeable pause before Alicia responded in clipped phrases. "Of course I do. I've always adored Carter. He and Jim were best friends. He wants to take care of the boys and me. He loves us and we adore him."

"I know, I know," Sloan had said, impatient with her friend's failure to see the point she was trying to make. "You've told me a hundred times how he and Jim grew up together, went to school together, how like brothers they were. But is that reason enough to marry him? He's not Jim, Alicia."

"That's cruel, Sloan, cruel! I'll never love anyone

the way I loved Jim, but I love Carter in a different way. Because of what Jason did to you, you're bitter and skeptical about any relationship between a man and a woman. That's why you've locked yourself away in that old house of yours and haven't looked at a man in the two years since that jerk jilted you."

Since her friend had been painfully correct, Sloan had apologized and let the subject drop. Carter and Alicia seemed to have come to amenable marriage terms. Far be it from her to presume to counsel anyone on matters of the heart.

Shaking herself out of her reverie, she said briskly, "I don't know why I've kept you standing in the hall. I'm sure you're ready to go up to your room."

"I have no complaints about your hospitality. After all, I got you out of bed. Is everyone else asleep?"

"Three of the six bedrooms are occupied and, yes, everyone went up after dinner." That statement seemed to underline the fact that they were alone together in the darkened hallway and that she was in her gown and robe, and barefoot. Nervously, a dainty pink tongue darted out to wet her lips. "Alicia said you'd want a large room with its own bath." She indicated the top of the stairs with a floundering hand. "It's the last door at the end of the hall."

He seemed disinclined to go up just yet. In any event he didn't move. "You weren't afraid to open your door to a man this late at night?"

"Alicia had described you. And I recognized you from the dust jacket picture on the back of your last book."

His eyebrows contributed to an exaggerated scowl. The brows weren't a matched pair. One arched eloquently while the other remained a straight bar over his eye with only a jagged crook at its inside end. "God, I hope not. My agent insisted on the Brooks Brothers suit. I think they even combed my hair before the picture was taken."

It wasn't combed now. The San Francisco fog had settled on it like a sparkling veil, drops occasionally beading on the deep russet strands that had fallen casually across his forehead and brushed his collar and the tops of his ears. He was agreeably shaggy. And the army green fatigue jacket had never seen the inside of Brooks Brothers. In fact, it looked like it had survived every war since the one of 1812. Nor had the faded jeans and scarred Adidas come from an exclusive haberdashery.

The glossy black and white picture that had gazed back at Sloan from the cover of *Parisian Escapade* was a two-dimensional parody of the face that was smiling at her now. She had sought out the book on her cluttered shelf yesterday in order to acquaint herself with this expected guest. Alicia could have done a lot worse, she had thought objectively. Once the book was replaced on the shelf, she hadn't given Carter Madison's appearance a thought.

The austere picture couldn't have prepared her for the flesh and blood version of his face. It was a rugged face that had enjoyed his thirty-four years— Alicia had told her how old he was. Laugh lines had been carved down either side of his mouth and there was a network of crinkles at the corners of his eyes. What had been a blandly smiling mouth in the photograph was lazily sensuous in reality, frequently unmasking a brilliant display of white teeth, slightly crooked on the bottom row. The nose that had conveyed a haughty condescension in the picture was in reality long and straight and . . . unpretentious.

His body hadn't seemed all that impressive beneath the Brooks Brothers suit. In the flesh, it made a woman want to touch it. It was hard and lean, intimating both power and grace. It was a tall, rangy physique, but without the slightest hint of clumsiness. It moved as if it knew exactly what it was doing and had been trained not to waste a motion.

"Where to?"

She whipped herself back into the immediacy of the situation. "Oh, your room is ready and I'm sure you're exhausted. Let me get a key." Grateful for an excuse not to look at him any longer, she turned toward her office at the back of the stairs. He halted her.

"I hate to trouble you any more than necessary, but I'm starving. They served peanuts on the flight. Is there a chance that a paying guest could coax a merciful hostess out of a bowl of cornflakes? Something? I'm not particular."

"I served pot roast for dinner. Would a roast beef sandwich suit you?"

"You're talking to a man who would have settled for cornflakes," he said, placing one hand over his heart.

Trying not to notice how adorable he was, Sloan said, "If you'll just have a seat in the dining room," she indicated the room to their left, "I'll bring it right out."

At the flip of a switch, the dining room was instantly bathed with a subtle light from the crystal chandelier. The table had already been set for breakfast, something she always did after the dinner dishes had been cleared away. The crystal reflected the soft light, the silver gleamed against the starched linen cloth, the china plates held napkins standing sentinel in their polished centers. Fresh flowers arranged in an antique soup tureen for a centerpiece added a perky touch of color and homeyness to the formality.

"All by myself?"

Turning around, she found him close behind her as he peered into the elegantly furnished room that was Sloan's pride and joy. He had dropped his eyeglasses onto the bridge of his nose. She liked the way he looked in them. "I don't—"

"Well, you've obviously set the table for breakfast. Wouldn't it be less trouble if I just ate my sandwich in the kitchen? Preferably off a paper plate?"

"No trouble," she breathed. He was so close and so much taller than she that she had to tilt her head back to look up at him. Her hand sneaked up the front of her robe, gathering material as it went until it clamped a damp wad of it at the base of her throat, hopefully to hide the erratic pulse beating there.

His eyes wandered over her face for a long moment, and the slender hand gripping the robe held his attention for an inordinate amount of time before he said softly. "Where's the kitchen?"

"This way." Even as she said it, Sloan knew that what she was doing was highly irregular. No guest had ever been in the kitchen. It was insane to initiate the practice with a single, male guest, yet it would have been ridiculous to stand there in the dark hallway, wearing no more than her bedclothes, insisting that he take a seat at the dining-room table. She shouldn't have given in to his request. She was the owner and manager, wasn't she? When had her authority disappeared?

But irrationally, it seemed the sensible thing to do to lead Carter down the hall. He had left his suitcase and typewriter at the foot of the stairs and was pulling off his jacket by the time they reached the kitchen.

Sloan turned on the light and fairly flew into getting him his snack. It included not only a sandwich, but leftover fruit salad, a piece of chocolate layer cake, and a tall glass of milk, which he said he preferred to coffee. She knew his eyes were following her as she flitted around the kitchen, intent on her chore and cursing her unaccountable nervousness. It was uncalled for. Reminding herself who he was and why he was here, she said, "Alicia didn't tell me David was playing soccer."

There. That was a safe topic. Somehow bringing Alicia's name into the room with them alleviated the intimacy of having him in her kitchen, at her small work table, eating the meal she had fixed exclusively for him in the middle of the night, while she sat across the table wondering if he knew she was naked beneath her gown.

What a stupid thing to worry about, Sloan. Everyone is naked beneath their clothes.

He swallowed a bite and took a long gulp of milk, wiping his mouth with a napkin before he responded, "They start them out young. And some of those little buggers can run."

"I'm sure it meant a lot to David for you to watch him play." She toyed with the sugar bowl in the center of the table. The room was chilly, the heat having economically been turned down when she'd finished working in there for the night. She hoped he didn't notice the tightening of her nipples and mistake the reason for it. To her, their hard distention was excruciatingly apparent. She couldn't have been more aware of them if a red neon arrow were pointing to them as if to say, "Look at me, I'm aroused, I'm aroused."

"Both he and Adam are cute kids, but they need a male influence. Both sets of grandparents are overindulgent. And Alicia finds it difficult to be firm. She's afraid stern discipline on top of Jim's death would damage their psyches or something."

"The accident was so horribly tragic. I'm certain they were traumatized not only by their father's death, but by the news it generated."

"No doubt." He banged his fist on the table. "Dammit, what was in Jim's head to be driving in that race in the first place? Gambling not only his life, but theirs, was foolhardy and selfish. When he proudly showed me that damned car of his, I advised him to get rid of it, begged him not to get serious about racing the thing." Sloan shared his sentiments, but she'd never spoken them aloud. "I know it sounds bad to say this, but I'm still mad as hell at him for doing such an irresponsible, rotten thing to Alicia and the boys."

He took another drink of milk and eyed her over the top of his glass. When he set it down he said, "It's funny that I was Jim's best friend and you're Alicia's and yet we've never met. Why weren't you at their wedding?"

She dragged her eyes from the corner of his mouth, a spot that continued to intrigue her. "Uh . . . I was in Egypt."

"You went all the way to Egypt just to avoid attending the wedding?"

She laughed. "No. My parents are Egyptologists. They coerced me into going on a three-month trip with them. Alicia threatened, cried, and pleaded, but there was no help for it. I'd promised my parents I'd go and it was too expensive to come back for the wedding."

Was he looking at her front? Yes, he was. *Oh, God.* As casually as she could, she crossed her arms over her chest.

"Did . . . did you like Egypt?" He seemed to have something stuck in his throat. His voice had become gravelly.

"It was all right." Actually she'd hated every minute she was there. It had been her parents' trip of a lifetime. Her father, a professor of history at UCLA, and her mother, who had been his research assistant before becoming his wife, had persuaded Sloan to travel with them.

As she'd feared, she'd been to them away from home what she was to them at home, an unpaid servant. She handled their travel arrangements, saw to their packing, their clothes, their appointments. As it had always been, when they weren't totally involved with their work, they were totally involved with each other to the exclusion of everything, even their daughter.

"What did you do before Fairchild House?"

She attributed his prying questions to his writer's curiosity. Her personal history would be boring to him and it was painful for her, so she kept her answers polite and general. "I worked for a company in Burbank that manufactures and markets office supplies."

"And you left all that for this beautiful old house in San Francisco?"

His eyes were teasing, dancing with amber lights.

"Well it *was* a tremendous sacrifice." She drew a sad face, then they laughed together. It felt good.

"How did you acquire the house?"

"It was almost an incidental item in my grandfather's will. My parents had no interest in it. I came up here to see it and knew at once what I wanted to do."

She had returned to Los Angeles, quit her job, notified her parents of the turn her life was going to take, and made the move all within a matter of weeks. "It took every penny of the money Grandfather had left me to have the place restored. It was in deplorable condition."

"But right off Union Street? My God, that was lucky."

"It was in the shadow of a ramshackle warehouse or I'm certain someone would have tried to buy it from us before then. Grandfather had owned it since the thirties, but it had been vacant for years. The warehouse has since been torn down. So I'm sitting on a prime piece of real estate, if the taxes are any indication. But in essence, it didn't cost me anything."

He glanced around the modernized kitchen that Sloan had had to redo from the foundation up. "You've done a remarkable job. The house is great."

"Thank you. Now if I can only keep my head above water until I start making a profit . . ." To complete her sentence, she crossed the fingers of both hands and squeezed her eyes shut. Carter laughed.

"I thought you'd be like Alicia. You're not."

Sloan was dismally aware of that. Alicia had been a campus beauty queen at UCLA when she and Sloan had become friends. Blonde, blue-eyed, rounded and dimpled, Alicia had often made Sloan feel like a diluted washout.

Sloan's hair was dark blond, threaded with lighter streaks in varying shades. Her eyes were the color of the sky seen through smoked glass. Sloan's figure was just as shapely as her friend's, but with all the excess flesh trimmed away.

"I don't think anyone could argue that," she said lightly now, trying to dismiss the thorough way Carter was looking at her as another characteristic of his career. Writers were constantly gathering material, weren't they? "Alicia's beautiful."

"So are you."

She bolted out of her chair and bumped her thighs bruisingly on the table in the process. "Thank you. Would you like something else?" she asked nervously, wishing her hands wouldn't tremble as she reached for his dishes. She didn't own a package of paper plates.

"No thank you. It was delicious."

She carried the dishes to the sink and ran water over them. "I'll take you to your room." She rushed past him, wishing she hadn't noticed how well his shirt fit his torso as he slung his jacket over his shoulder or how his jeans molded to the muscles of his thighs and the bulge of his sex.

God, she was becoming a frustrated old maid with her mind only on one thing.

"I hope your room is satisfactory," Sloan said over her shoulder as she led him back the way they'd come and then to her office under the stairs. Opening a cabinet where labeled keys were neatly hung on cuphooks, she took one down and dropped it into his hand. She dared not touch him.

"Does it have a table I can set my typewriter on?"

"I moved one in there for you . . . and a chair."

"Thank you. I can't tell you how wonderful it's going to be to get in some uninterrupted work."

"I wondered why you couldn't finish your book in LA. Alicia said that's where the two of you will be living. I assumed you had a place there."

"I do. Right on the beach. Lovely place. It has everything."

"Then—"

"Including a telephone. And everyone has the number. Alicia's mother calls and asks if I know what color dress my mother plans to wear to the wedding. When I suggest she call her she says, 'Oh, but I hate to bother her.' Then Alicia's father calls and asks me to lunch to meet some of his friends and I tell him I'm working and he says, 'But you have to eat sometime.' And then Alicia calls and then David and then Adam and—"

"Little Adam?" Sloan asked, laughing as he verbally painted a truly frustrating picture. "He's only three."

"But he knows how to dial my number." He shook his head. "I can't yell at any of them. They don't realize how distracting those interruptions are to my train of thought."

"What about after you're married and have to work? It won't get any easier."

"Yes, but *then* I can yell."

They laughed softly together for a moment, and when it subsided that sense of intimacy came between them once more, making them each aware of the other.

"Well there aren't any telephones in the rooms here," Sloan said breathlessly.

"It's sounding more ideal by the minute."

"Alicia said you'd be working almost all the time."

She hoped that frantic note in her voice went past him undetected. "I believe you have only the last chapter to go."

They were at the foot of the stairs now, but he made no move to pick up either the suitcase or the typewriter. When he'd been eating, his eyeglasses had remained perched on his head. Now, he flopped them down over his eyes again, but rather than to facilitate his seeing, it was so he could rake a hand through his dry, but no less disheveled hair. "Yeah, but it's a killer."

"Don't you know how the book is going to end?" One hand rested on the oak bannister that, after hours of elbow grease had been applied, shone with a warm patina. The other fiddled awkwardly with the tie of her robe at her waist. It was quiet, their voices hushed. She wished she couldn't see the wedge of dark hair beneath his partially unbuttoned shirt. She wished even more that the desire to touch it had never sparked in her mind.

"Yes, but I've got to do the scene where the hero overcomes the villain and the last love scene between the two protagonists."

"That shouldn't be too difficult when you're able to concentrate. You're very good with the suspense scenes, and I'm sure that with a title like *Sleeping Mistress* the love scene will be no problem."

His grin was wide. "But the sleeping mistress isn't a woman."

"It's a *man*?" she asked, aghast.

He hooted a laugh and at her 'Shhhhh,' reduced it to a contrite, silent chuckle. "Not with a Carter Madison hero," he said, trying to look offended. "No, the word mistress refers to his sense of duty. It's his passion, what drives him, what makes him tick. It fades from importance when he meets the heroine and he no longer lets it govern his decisions. It doesn't reassert itself until the final pages."

She didn't realize she had become trapped between him and the wall until she felt it against the back of her head as she looked up at him. "So he'll have to give up the woman?"

He shrugged, his eyes scouring her face in the shadows. She could feel his breath on her skin, warm and fragrant. She wanted to taste it. "I think I'll have to leave it up to the hero to make that decision. And then there's the heroine to consider. Would a woman love a man freely when she knows it's against all odds and that nothing can come of it?"

Just in time, Sloan kept herself from acting on an impulse to cover her breasts which were suddenly full and aching. "Maybe she won't love him freely. Maybe he'll force her."

He shook his head, though his eyes never left hers. "No. He's the hero, remember. Heroes never have to resort to rape. Besides, he knows she feels the same ambiguity that he does."

"Does she?"

"I'm almost sure of it."

"So the ending will be sad?"

"Bittersweet at best."

"I don't think I'll want to read it."

"You may have to help me write it."

By now, he was so close she could feel the heat his body generated. She could see her frightened, inquiring reflection in his eyeglasses as he bent over her. She saw her lips part invitingly, saw her lashes lower until her eyes took on the sultry expression of a woman about to be kissed.

Cruelly, conscience yanked her out of the sensuous web their conversation had spun around them. She squeezed between him and the wall, trying desperately not to touch him, to gain the first stair.

"I'll take you up now," she wheezed.

"Sloan." Had he not closed strong fingers around her wrist to detain her, his speaking her name for the first time would have accomplished it just as effectively. Her name sounded like poetry coming from his lips. She looked first at his fingers locked closed around her wrist, then up at his face. "I'm perfectly capable of finding the last room at the end of the hall," he said after they had looked at each other for a heart-stopping long while. "No need for you to bother."

"Then I'll see you at breakfast." Could he feel the pulse racing beneath the pad of his thumb? "I serve between seven-thirty and nine-thirty."

"In bed?"

Her throat closed as tightly as the fingers around her wrist, which hadn't modified their hold one bit. She imagined them closing just as firmly over her throbbing breasts and giving them relief. The muscular breakdown in her thighs was a delicious sensation, like having melted butter dripped on them. "What do you mean?"

"Do you serve breakfast in bed?"

"If . . . if a guest prefers not to come down to the dining room, I can bring a tray to his . . . her . . . their room."

"I prefer."

Chapter Two

Carter stood in the bay window of his room, watching the morning spread over the fabulous city of San Francisco. From this window, he could see to the corner of Union Street where fashionable boutiques, galleries, and restaurants lined the sidewalks. There was no sun today. Only a lighter wash of pale gray brightened the landscape as the minutes ticked by. The weather didn't match his mood.

He'd never felt sunnier in his life.

And the bubbling wellspring of happiness in his chest made him feel guilty as hell, more despicable than the vilest blackguard to ever grace the pages of the most gruesome fairy tale.

He glanced over his bare shoulder at the bed that still showed the imprint of his body on its pastel sheets. He'd slept like a rock, like a man who didn't have a guilty conscience. Not that it hadn't taken him a helluva long time to fall asleep. It had. But once he'd faced the fact that the image of her face wasn't going to fade and that there wasn't a damn thing he could do about it, his eyes had closed peacefully and he'd slept like a log. When he'd awakened, he could feel the silly, satisfied grin on his face and was immediately ashamed of it. He hadn't been dreaming of Alicia.

Work. That's what he needed. Hard, frustrating, soul-gripping, mind-wrenching, emotion-draining work. Regretfully leaving the window, he went to the small square table which had been set up in the middle of the room and hauled his typewriter onto it. When it had been uncovered, when he'd meticulously placed a fresh stack of paper beside it, when the box containing the four hundred and some odd pages of his unfinished manuscript had been set at his right hand to receive the pages he intended to rip out with unprecedented ease, when he'd adjusted his glasses on his nose, he sat down in the chair. And stared into space.

God! Had he ever in his thirty-four years been poleaxed by the sight of a woman as he'd been last night? No. He was sure of that. He would have remembered.

She had looked so damned cute standing there with her messed up hair and bare feet. The robe was horrible, pale blue and woolly, something a cold-natured grandmother would wear. Beneath it he could see the hem of a pale yellow nylon nightgown. The ensemble couldn't have enticed a lustful deviate, yet he'd felt the first stirrings in his loins even then.

She had ceased to be "cute" after he'd followed her into the kitchen. When she'd bent down to take a linen napkin out of a drawer and he'd seen no demarcating lines panties would have made on a perfectly wonderful tush, he'd stopped thinking of her as cute and started speculating on the lithe, slender female form beneath that offensive blue shroud.

He'd had a helluva time getting that sandwich

past the knot in his throat. Especially when he noticed the twin peaks trying their best to poke through the front of her robe. God, he'd almost choked on the bite he'd just taken. He'd had no illusions as to why her nipples were contracted. It certainly wasn't because of his devastating effect on women. Simply put, it had been cold in the room. That was all. But the effect had been the same and the cause hadn't made it any easier for him to keep his eyes, much less his hands, off her breasts.

Appealing though her body was, it was her eyes that had enchanted him the most. They were beautiful, a subtle shade of blue overlaid with grey. He was sure she wasn't aware of all they revealed about her. There was sadness lurking in those eyes. Pain. Hurt. Wariness. She was like a small animal that had been beaten one too many times and was afraid to venture out again.

That fearful caution had been thrown into high gear just before he'd come upstairs. That frightened look was probably the only thing that had kept him from kissing her. Kissing, hell. Her expression was the only thing that had kept him from doing anything she was willing to let him get away with.

Because by that time, he'd almost forgotten who Alicia was. Desire, hot and rampant, had filled him, hardened him, until he thought he would burst if he didn't touch her. His heart had been pounding in his ears, drowning out every word of chastisement his conscience was blaring. Conscience, duty, responsibility, morality. To hell with all that. For that moment his whole being had been under carnal rule and it had taken that fear in her eyes to keep him from acting on it.

Now, he pushed out of his chair and circled the table like a caged cat, wiping his hands on the legs of his jeans because even the recollection of how much he'd wanted to touch her had caused them to perspire again.

"You randy bastard," he growled to himself. Because if he didn't know anything else about her, he knew that Sloan Fairchild was a decent woman and would probably die of mortification if she had known what was going through his mind. "You're engaged to her best friend, for godsakes," he reminded himself with disgust. "You're committed, ol' buddy."

He thought he might well be committed in an entirely different manner of speaking if he spent the whole month under Sloan's roof.

The manuscript seemed to call to him from the desk. "Right," he answered as if he'd been sternly castigated. "That's the reason I'm here. To work."

He linked his hands, turned them inside out, and stretched, then sat back down at the table. He stared at the blank sheet of paper and rested his hands on the keys. Unbidden, a sudden inspiration occurred to him. What would the character in his book have done had he arrived on the doorstep of a beautiful woman in dishabille in the middle of the night?

"Stupid question," Carter said self-derisively. "That's fiction. Anything can happen that you say happens."

He gave his mind free rein. Had he been Gregory, the hero, instead of Carter Madison, a decent enough fellow who usually obeyed his conscience, he'd have followed the winsome Ms. Fairchild into her kitchen. The moment he saw her nipples straining against the front of her robe, he'd have reached across the table and covered one with his palm, massaging it with a slow, measured circular motion until it was as round and hard as a pearl.

This is lunacy, Carter, his conscience warned him. *It doesn't matter. This is fantasy, that's all,* his libido argued back. *Besides you can't be hanged for what you're thinking.*

Gregory would have swept the table clear with one fell swoop of his hand, grabbed her up and—

No, no, no. That's got no finesse. No class.

The floor? Too cold. Again, no class.

Wait, I've got it! He'd have slowly drawn her to her feet. She'd have been shy, reluctant, and put up a temporary show of resistance. But as soon as his lips met hers, she'd have molded against him. His arms would have closed tight around her. Kissing her intimately, sliding his tongue into her mouth like a sword into its sheath, he'd have backed them to the counter, where he'd have lifted her up. She would have murmured a sigh of protest when he untied the robe, but she would have allowed it. Then slowly his hands would part it and he'd see . . . the yellow nightgown that was probably as chaste and ugly as the robe.

"Dammit," Carter said aloud and cursed himself. He dug into his eyesockets with the heels of his hands, determined to concentrate on Gregory and his problems, but Carter's problem was throbbing beneath his tight jeans and wouldn't be ignored.

This is your fantasy, you fool. Pretend there was no nightgown. Pretend she was . . .

Then slowly his hands would part it and he'd see . . . her naked breasts, heaving with longing, tipped with coral nipples that responded to the merest breath of stimulation. He'd touch them as he continued kissing her. Stroke them. Tease them. Then he'd lower his head and take one into his mouth and suck it gently. She'd be virtually wild by now, making low gutteral noises in her throat, and curling her legs around him. And when he drew back and outlined the button shape of her nipple with the tip of his tongue, she'd reach for—

"Mr. Madison?"

"What!?" he shouted as he cannoned out of his chair, knocking it over along with the stack of papers that flew in every direction when he spun around. He practically broke the stem of his eyeglasses when he whipped them off.

Sloan was standing just inside the door, a large silver tray covered with a cloth balanced on one hand, her other still gripping the doorknob as though his fierce response had welded it there.

She wet her lips in the nervously reflexive way he was coming to recognize. He tried to blink eyes dilated with passion back into focus, tried to capture lost breath that remained elusive, and tried to pretend that his loins still weren't on fire. He also tried to pretend that he wasn't base enough to bring a lady like Sloan Fairchild into a sordid, lewd fantasy. He succeeded at none of those endeavors.

"I . . . I knocked," she said in a high, timid voice.

"I'm sorry, Sloan. I was . . . uh . . . deep in thought. Here, let me." He took long strides toward the door and a spasm of regret crossed his face when he saw her flinch with precaution. He attempted to lighten the situation. "I guess I scared you to death, yelling like that. I apologize again."

"When you didn't answer my knock, I got worried and . . ."

He relieved her of the tray, but he didn't move away. Instead they stood like statues in the frame of the doorway and stared at each other. That wariness was still in her eyes and his originally sunny mood clouded to become as gloomy as the day.

He could fantasize all he wanted to, but the reality wouldn't go away. He was engaged to a woman and two little boys who needed him. He'd never had passionate fantasies about Alicia, but they shared a different kind of love. Perhaps it was the safest kind. It certainly didn't bring one from the height of bliss to the pits of despair in a matter of seconds.

Love? What the hell was he talking about? He'd been reading too many of his own books. Love didn't happen this quickly. Sometimes it took years to develop between two people. But as he saw the confusion swirling in the smoky depths of Sloan's eyes, he knew she had been poleaxed, too. God only knew what they were going to do about it.

"You'd better eat this while it's hot." She indicated the tray with a nod of her head. When he hadn't answered her knock, why hadn't she gone back downstairs and tried again later? Possibly he would have pulled on a shirt by then. As it was, all he wore now was a pair of jeans. The sight of his naked chest was doing nothing to eliminate the vertigo she'd been subjected to since she first saw him.

He turned away and she let loose the pent-up breath she'd been holding. She was glad she could no longer see that wide chest forested with dark, curly hair. It swirled over the contoured muscles and lay sleek and glossy against the plain of his stomach and then tapered to a fine satiny line down into his pants.

"Join me?"

"No," she said too loudly and too quickly. He was pulling on a shirt, thank God. His back had been smooth, the muscles rippling beneath tanned skin. It had been almost as tempting to touch as his chest. At his surprised look, she tempered her reply. "No, thank you. The other guests are in the dining room. I have to be on hand if they need something."

"And I don't deserve the same attention?"

The arching brow that couldn't seem to keep still no matter what the mood was dancing with mirth. He was teasing her, being deliberately provoking, and her frazzled nerves couldn't handle it. "Yes," she said with a touch of asperity. "But it should be obvious that I can't be two places at once and since they are six and you are one, majority rules. *You* requested the tray in your room. Maybe you should reconsider next time. And, I don't think my other guests would like the idea of their hostess sharing a room with a single male guest. I'll be back later to pick up the tray."

She was convinced that she hadn't slammed the door behind her, but the rattle of the windows said otherwise. "This is all Alicia's fault," she muttered as she smoothed her prim chignon with her hand in the classic gesture of a distressed woman trying to regain her composure. She vowed with each step down the stairs that she'd throttle her friend the next time she saw her.

What was wrong with Alicia? Was she dense? To send a man who looked like Carter to a woman, any woman, was lunacy. Didn't she know he'd attract women like fish to bait? And no matter how good a friend Sloan was, and no matter how dull and dependable and trustworthy she was, she wasn't dead. And that's the only kind of woman who could be immune to Carter Madison's appeal.

Just beyond the archway into the dining room, Sloan paused to draw in several restorative breaths and paint on a gracious hostess smile before she went in. "More orange muffins for everyone?"

"Yes," they chorused.

When she came from the kitchen bearing another basket of muffins, she offered to pack some in a sack for the couple who were leaving that morning. "You can munch on them in the car."

"Why how lovely of you, Miss Fairchild. Thank you." The couple was from Maine and they had driven cross-country to the west coast. They planned to start the long trek back that day. "Ernest and I have enjoyed our stay with you so much."

Sloan smiled. "Then I hope you'll suggest Fairchild House to your friends who plan to visit San Francisco."

"We certainly will," Ernest said around his mouthful of orange muffin.

The two retired lady schoolteachers were staying until the end of the week. The banker and his wife were leaving the day after tomorrow. Sloan mentally tabulated how much their tabs would add up to and only hoped it would be enough to pay her utility bills. When she had refilled everyone's coffee cup, she went back into the kitchen to sip at her own.

In the nine months Fairchild House had been open, she'd survived only by word of mouth. Just when she'd think she'd be forced to close, someone would call at the recommendation of a previous guest. There were several well-known bed and breakfast houses in San Francisco, but Sloan's was the newest. By next spring, she hoped to have ads running in travel magazines and the Sunday editions of major city newspapers. In the meantime, she was living on a shoestring, barely breaking even, but she was surviving.

At the time she'd left her boring job and moved to San Francisco, that had been her main objective: to survive. Her engagement to Jason Hubbard had come to a crushing, irrevocable termination. Her parents sadly lamented her disappointment in love and then returned to their dusty books and charts, turning their minds away from their daughter's dismal life to the intriguing one of a pharaoh. She loved her parents with a resigned fondness, and she knew if asked they would say they loved her. But around them she rarely felt like more than a convenient servant when they needed her to see to the rudiments of life, or a nuisance who didn't share their passion for ancient history when she tried to direct the conversation to any other topic. Their affection was sincere when they happened to look up, see her, and remember that she existed.

In short, no one cared what she did with the rest of her life. Not her parents. Not Jason—laughing, handsome Jason—who had stolen her heart, her virginity, then one night blithely told her she was too staid, that he needed someone with more energy, more excitement. Only she had known that if she stayed where she was, doing what she was doing, she'd vegetate.

It hadn't been easy, but with the money her grandfather had willed her, her degree in business from UCLA, her love of cooking, and a wish and a prayer, she'd undertaken to make something of Fairchild House. She'd acquired a knowledge of antiques by poring over books at night. Estate sales became her passion and when she wasn't wielding a paintbrush or papering walls, she was dashing off to one with hopes of finding something both pretty and serviceable. Slowly but surely, the rooms of the house had been furnished.

She took secret pride in what she'd accomplished even if no one else had noticed. Other women had a man, children, to occupy their lives. They could afford to be romantic, impractical, and sometimes irresponsible. Because they knew their man would take care of them.

Sloan had to be pragmatic, frugal and dependable. Since birth, since she first realized that her parents had relinquished their duty the moment she was brought home from the hospital, she'd learned to fend for herself. It did no good to wish that just once, before she became the dried-up old woman she knew she was destined to be, she could know what it felt like to be cherished. What was the point of dreaming for something that could never be? Why waste precious energy on wondering why she was so unlovable?

This morning her deficiencies where romance was concerned seemed more deficient than usual.

Could her despondency have something to do with the weather? Or was its source the man upstairs? But then that was unthinkable. He belonged to her best friend and even if he didn't, a man of his caliber, his world-wide notoriety, would never be attracted to someone like her.

Nevertheless, it took a long time before she built up enough courage to retrieve his breakfast tray.

She tapped softly on the door, halfway hoping that he wouldn't answer or that he'd snarl at her that he was busy and would she please go away. Instead his "Come in" came through the door clearly.

"I'm sorry to bother you while you're working," she said as she entered. "I know you don't like distractions."

He wasn't working. He was standing at the window. His hands had been turned backward and stuffed into the back pockets of his jeans. Tight as they were, she would have thought that impossible. He had finished dressing. His shirt was buttoned—at least *most* of the buttons were fastened. He was wearing the same pair of running shoes as last night. He had showered. The room smelled of masculine soap and a brisk cologne. His jaw looked recently shaved. Though his hair was still damp from washing, it looked like it had been combed by aggravated hands.

"I'm not working," he said scornfully, tilting his head toward the papers he'd scattered earlier. Added to them were numerous balled up sheets. His eyeglasses lay neglected beside the empty typewriter. The chair had been righted but sat askew from the desk. "Are you armed and dangerous this time?" The roguish eyebrow climbed up his forehead.

He was referring to her tart departing speech

and she blushed hotly. "I'm sorry if I sounded cross, but really, Mr. Madison, I'm not—"

"Sloan, please cut the Mr. Madison crap. I'm Carter, okay?" He looked thoroughly agitated. The hands came out of his pockets and he ground one fist into the palm of the other.

Sloan felt the first signals of irritation starting in her chest. "All right then, *Carter*, if you'll allow me to get the tray, which I'm sure is in your way, I'll leave you alone and let you start work again."

Erect and proud, she stamped to the table, covered the now empty plates with the linen cloth, and began lifting it. She saw his arm come from around her and the large, strong hand still hers.

"I'm sorry," was a low, vibrating rumble close to her ear. It sent chills racing up and down her arm, over her whole body, to be followed by an unbearable tide of heat. "I don't expect any special treatment. The breakfast was superb."

His hand had been withdrawn, but still she couldn't move. "Thank you."

"The room is charming."

"Thank you."

"I slept better than I have in weeks."

"I'm glad." *These two word sentences are really terrific, Sloan. Keep it up and he'll soon be nodding off.* It was just that her brain and mouth had lost all contact with each other. She couldn't form a more coherent, loquacious response. Not when he was standing only a hair's breadth away.

"Forgive my foul mood. Not that I don't want you to stop calling me Mr. Madison. I do. But I'm a bear when I'm trying to write and nothing's there. The words just won't come."

In the small space he had allowed her, she turned around and found herself gazing up into the sherry-colored facets of his eyes. "Why not? Is it a rough spot?"

For the sake of his tenuous sanity, he took a step back. It was all he could do to keep from touching her. "Yeah. I've hit a snag. Why did you pin your hair up like that?"

The two sentences were so unrelated that it took a moment for her to grasp his meaning. When she did, her hand flew to the bun on the back of her neck. "Is there something wrong with it?" she asked out of female vanity. Were pins showing? Had she left out a strand?

"No, no. Nothing's wrong. It's just that, well, I liked it better last night. Sort of loose and . . . wild . . . sexy."

She swallowed hard and dragged her eyes away from the magnetic power of his. "Well, wild and sexy isn't the way guests want the hostess of a bed and breakfast house to be."

"I bet you haven't polled the male guests." His eyes were sparkling again with teasing lights. She didn't know which was more dangerous, when they were smoldering, as a moment ago, or like now when they were boyishly mischievous. Both seemed to have a devastating effect on her equilibrium.

She drew herself up straight, turned back to the table, and said hurriedly. "I must get to work—"

"Wait!" he cried sharply and she spun around in surprise. "Maybe you can help me here a minute."

"With what?"

"With my book."

"I don't know anything about writing."

"Not writing. I need a female body to handle."

Probably she'd have been wise to look affronted, rapidly gather up the tray, and huff out. Instead she laughed. "I'm sure you don't mean that the way it sounded."

He looked chagrined and laughed himself. "Perhaps I should rephrase that. Gregory is trying to get information out of the heroine, see?"

"Who is Gregory?"

"The hero. And—"

"What's her name?"

"Lisa. So he gets in a tussle with her and she's struggling. But he loves this girl and he doesn't want to hurt her. I need a woman's body to see how tough a man can get to make his point and still not hurt her. See?"

"Wouldn't that depend on the woman? I mean, if she's a health enthusiast, a lady wrestler, or skilled in martial arts, she's obviously not going to be hurt too easily."

"No. Lisa's soft and feminine. Slender. Like you."

Her hand fluttered to her throat to self-consciously pat at her collar. "What . . ." She cleared her throat. "What do you want me to do?"

He took her hand and pulled her away from the table. "Let's go over here where we have more room. I don't want to knock over any of your antique china." He faced her and released her hand, shaking his muscles loose like a boxer in the ring waiting for the match to begin. "Okay, I've just called you a tramp—actually a little stronger word than tramp—who would sell your body to both sides if the price were right."

"And you're supposed to love me?" She shook her head, not believing what she'd just said. "I mean, he's supposed to love her?"

"He does, but he's mad as hell because she knows something that will help him get the bad guys, but she's protecting the uncle who has raised her and is being threatened by the bad guys." He took a deep, excited breath. "So, I've called you this terrible name and since you've made love with me on numerous occasions, you're doubly insulted."

Sloan was made uneasy by his putting the story into the first person. She'd have preferred the characters be referred to as Gregory and Lisa, but she nodded her understanding anyway.

"Come at me intending to slap me."

She glanced down at the floor, deliberately trying to throw him off guard, then lunged at him with her hand raised. The next thing she knew she'd been spun around and slammed into his chest. The hand she'd raised was being held between her shoulder blades in a twisting grip while the other was pinioned between their torsos. His other arm was against her throat while a hand like iron closed over her shoulder. His hard cheek lay along hers as he pressed her head onto his shoulder. The chignon on the back of her head had come down.

"Carter," she gasped in outraged surprise, trying to extricate herself. "Let me go."

"Am I hurting you?"

She drew in great gulps of air. "You don't play fair. You didn't warn me you were going to do this."

"I'm sorry, but that's just how Lisa would have felt. I had to get a realistic physical reaction from you. Am I hurting you?" he repeated.

She analyzed herself. "No," she answered truthfully. He wasn't hurting her, but there was no means of escape that she could see either. She pitied poor Lisa. If Gregory were anything like Carter, his appealing closeness was as deadly as his stranglehold.

"What are you feeling?"

She was feeling that if he didn't stop grinding the fly of his jeans into her derriere, she was going to faint. "Frightened." That was the most honest answer she could give him. The sensations he had engendered inside her were terrifying.

"Even though you know I love you and really don't want to hurt you?"

"Yes," she breathed and closed her eyes. "Don't violence and passion sometimes run hand in hand?"

God, why was he punishing her this way? His legs were as hard and long as tree trunks against the back of hers. His breath in her ear was causing delightful things to happen to her breasts and between her thighs. For a woman as deprived of affection as she, it was like chaining a starving person in sight of a gourmet banquet and denying him the feast. Sloan's chains of conscience and loyalty to a friend were too strong to break easily, but that made her no less hungry.

"If you were Lisa, what would you do?"

If she were Lisa, she'd probably tell him everything he wanted to know and then beg him to take her. But that wasn't what he wanted to hear, so she willed her mind out of sensuous ponderings and tried to concentrate on the strictly physical. "I don't know. I'd probably struggle, if for no other reason than stung pride."

"Okay, stuggle."

Her movements were tentative at first, then more earnest. She couldn't budge him, and her efforts only resulted in rubbing their bodies together in a way that was both exquisite and horrifying. Her blouse worked its way out of her waistband. Her skirt became tangled around her legs. Her hair spilled down her neck. And her hand, which was still trapped between them, had accidentally, but indisputably, confirmed that his fly buttoned instead of zipped. "It's no use," she panted, only partially from exertion. "I can't get loose."

"You'll tell me everything I want to know?"

Her head dropped forward in defeat and she nodded meekly. Slowly his arms relaxed and he gradually released her. As soon as she was free, she whirled around and drove her heel down on his instep like a piston.

He cried out in pain and surprise, but recovered before she could run past him. He caught both her shoulders and shoved her down on the bed, following with his own body in a shallow dive. They grappled, Sloan struggling sincerely now, for he was positioned over her in a way that gratified their sexes. He too, was doing his best to gain the advantage and finally managed to catch both her flailing hands and haul them over her head.

With their labored breathing filling the quiet room, he lay his head next to hers and rested, never letting his fist around her wrists slacken. At last he raised his face only inches above hers.

"Very good," he conceded with a wry smile. "You almost got away."

It felt good, so good, to have his weight pressing her into the mattress. Each time she drew a rattling breath, her breasts rose and flattened against the unyielding wall of his chest. Having thrashed during their struggle, her legs now lay in humbled repose, parted slightly. He was a hard, full pressure between her thighs. Like an electrical connection that wasn't quite complete, sparks shot from that spot and showered them both with pinpricks of delight.

"After you subdue me, do I tell you the information you demanded?"

His eyes rained liquid fire over her features. "Yes," he said gruffly. "Eventually."

"And then what happens?" Her voice was as unsteady and low pitched as his.

His eyes slid down her throat, lower, to the place where the top two buttons of her blouse had come undone in their scuffle. Creamy breasts swelled over the lace-edged cups of her brassiere. He squeezed his eyes shut and tried not to envision his lips pressed into that velvety valley, tried not to imagine his tongue tracing that curved trail of lace or, having passed its boundaries, touching her nipple. When he opened his eyes and lifted his head to hers, he saw that smoky quality in her eyes and knew that her thoughts were the same as his.

"They make love," he whispered.

Their eyes fused in an understanding that would remain unspoken. A sob issued out of her throat, but whether out of anguish, or guilt, or self-denial, neither could have said. He levered himself up and she came off the bed with a bound. She kept her back to him as she straightened her clothes and pulled the dangling pins from her hair, shoving them into her skirt pocket as though she were hiding evidence. The best that could be done to her hair was done with trembling hands. She heard the scrape of the chair as he sat down. Within seconds he was rolling a sheet of paper into the typewriter and then the keys began to tap rhythmically.

If he could act as though nothing had happened, so could she. Going back to the bed, she began to smooth the linens. It cost her dearly to touch the pillow that was still cratered with the imprint of his head. When the bed was made, she cautiously walked toward the table and picked up the tray.

"Thank you for your assistance," he said quietly. He was wearing his glasses again.

"You're welcome. Did it help?"

"I think so. On the other hand it may have hurt."

"How so?"

He shook his head. "Never mind," he said through tense lips.

"I'll be going out for a while. Lunch isn't included with the room, but I can make you—"

"Where are you going?"

"To . . . to the wharf to buy some crab for dinner."

He vaulted out of the chair happily. "I'll go with you."

Chapter Three

"You can't." Her objection was so vehement, they were both surprised.

"Why not?" he asked, not quite successful in suppressing his amusement.

Her mind groped for a plausible reason. It should have been immediately obvious. "You have to work. That's why you're here, to get in hours of uninterrupted work."

"But even best-selling authors"—he executed a courtly bow—"deserve a day off." His smile was so warm, she could feel her heart melting beneath its glow. "I haven't quite got the feel of the place yet, know what I mean?" he said, glancing around the room. "It's a strange environment. Not that it's not lovely," he rushed to add. "It is. It's just not home yet, and I'm finding it hard to adjust, to concentrate, to tune out the strange surroundings."

That was all hogwash and she knew it, and he knew she knew it. He pressed on, trying a different tack to see if it sounded more believable. "My legs need stretching. I was in the plane and then in the cab all night last night. At least it seemed that way. I need the brisk bay air to sweep out the cobwebs. Besides I've always loved the wharf area. It will stimulate me."

Sloan thought that stimulation was the last thing he needed, but she couldn't voice that objection because she would be admitting that she knew he desired her. That was as good as admitting that his desire was reciprocated. Hopefully, if they both ignored it, it would go away.

"Really, Carter, if you want to go, I think you should go by yourself. I have several errands to run and—"

"And an extra pair of hands would come in handy," he finished for her. "Let me get my jacket."

Her usual astuteness failed her, and she couldn't think fast enough to manufacture another reason for him not to go with her. They didn't need another reason when the prevalent one was prohibitive enough. They shouldn't be playing with fire when obviously one ignited every time they were together. It was too late, however. He had already yanked the fatigue jacket from a hanger in the closet and pulled open the door to his room. "Should I lock it?"

"Yes. I have to lock the main door when I leave. I warned everyone this morning that I'd be out for a few hours so they wouldn't plan to return while the door was locked. But it never hurts to take extra precautions."

"You should have an assistant so you wouldn't have to stay here all the time," he remarked as they were trooping down the stairs.

"That would be nice and much more convenient, but unfortunately I can't afford a payroll." At the bottom of the stairs, she said, "I'll be right back."

Gaining her room, she hastily made repairs on her makeup. After raking a brush through her hair and taking the pins from her pocket, she found the thick strands unwilling to be contorted back into their neat bun. "To hell with it," she muttered under her breath, deciding to let it fall freely. The wind on the wharf would wreak havoc with it anyway. At least that's how she justified leaving it down. Her skirt and blouse were a bit rumpled, but would suffice. She pulled on a poplin jacket the color of the blue-grey fog that rolled into the bay from the ocean at dusk, grabbed up her purse, and checked to see that she had her shopping list.

Carter was leaning against the bannister with ankles and arms crossed waiting for her, "Ready?" she asked. She didn't miss the appreciative glance he gave her hair before she led him out the door, locking it behind her. The tiny garage attached to the side of the house would hold a car no larger than her compact. "Climb in," she said.

"You gotta be kiddin'," he said dryly. "Squeeze maybe, but not climb."

She couldn't keep from laughing as he sat down on the passenger side and pulled first one long leg, then the other between his seat and the dashboard.

She was accustomed to the perilously steep streets and the San Franciscan drivers who treated traffic lights as flashing decorations to be disregarded when at all possible. When she pulled into a coveted parking space near Fisherman's Wharf, Carter was a trifle pale, making three freckles on his cheekbone stand out starkly. "Are we here? I hope."

Sloan laughed at him. "Come on. As long as you insisted on tagging along, you can make yourself useful."

He helped her pick out the freshest, whitest crabmeat, sworn to have been brought in with the latest catch. She made her other necessary stops as they walked along the wharf, but she was often distracted.

"Come look at this, Sloan," he would call. Or, "Wait, let's go in here. I've been in this gallery before and it's terrific."

While she tried to make it seem like the outing were for business alone, she had the distinct impression that given half a chance, Carter would have made it into a lark.

When she accused him of that as she guiltily bit into her Ghirardelli chocolate bar, he said, "How often do you get out? I mean for fun and relaxation, not on an errand for Fairchild House." He was unselfconsciously slurping a gooey sundae as they sat at a small round table in the atrium room of the ice cream parlor.

"Not too often," she said dismissively.

"How often?" he persisted.

She fiddled with her candy wrapper. "I'm the sole owner and manger of Fairchild House. House-keeper, hostess, accountant, chief cook and bottle washer. That doesn't leave much time for fun and relaxation as you put it."

"You mean you never take a day off? An evening off? Never to go a movie? Nothing?"

"You're depressing me," she said, trying desperately to tease him away from the subject. Her life was far from a carnival, she just didn't want him to know how very dull it was.

"Sloan, that's ridiculous." He lay his spoon aside and studied her with embarrassing intentness.

"It's not ridiculous if there's no help for it."

"Hire some help."

"I can't afford it," she snapped. "I told you that earlier."

"You can't afford to hole up in that house and never come out, either," he flared back. When he saw her stricken expression, he lowered his voice. "I'm sorry. It's none of my business, of course, it's just that I can't understand why a beautiful woman like you would hide herself from the rest of the human race." He tapped his spoon on the table-top and wouldn't look at her when he asked quietly, "Don't you ever go out with men?"

"Rarely." Liar, she accused herself. "Never" would have been the appropriate answer.

He looked up at her again and she knew with a woman's instinct that he was thinking about what had happened between them that morning on the bed. "Has there ever been a man?"

"Yes," she said softly. Why keep the poor man in suspense? He was apparently dying to know all the gory details of her life. "We worked for the same company in L.A. He was a minor executive in charge of sales. He was very much a salesman, with impeccable taste in clothes, perfect manners, the gift of gab, and lots of shiny white teeth."

She took a drink of ice water. "I had just gradua-ted from UCLA, had just moved into my own apartment, was feeling independent and dedicated to succeeding in my career. I think he must have originally considered me a challenge, me with my dour determination. He made me laugh, relax, have a good time. In turn, I was good for him. I had new insight into what the public wanted. I listened and made suggestions when he was trou-bled about a particular product. In all modesty I think my ideas proved workable."

"No doubt."

"After a while, he"—she paused to wet her lips—"he had more of his things in my apartment than in his. I saw no reason not to share an apartment since we planned to marry."

She could have told her ardent listener that Jason had grown impatient with her "middle-class hang-ups" as he had called them. What woman came out of UCLA or Podunk U, for that matter, still clinging to her virginity like it was some pre-cious treasure? He had made her cry, because archaic as her thinking was, she *did* value her body and hadn't wanted to barter it off. A born saleman, he had finally convinced her that it would be selfish not to grant him what he wanted.

He'd been a frequent and fervent lover, but Sloan had always felt she were missing something. Every time they made love, he would want to know how he'd been, if his performance was up to par. She had smiled and said yes, but apparently her qualified answers weren't enough for his ego and he became more and more impatient for her to give him a rave review. But Sloan couldn't lie and say the sky opened up and heaven fell each time, because it hadn't. Never had. Never did. She knew there must be something desperately wrong with her.

So Jason had moved out. He took his hamster and the diamond ring on her left hand with him. She felt the former had meant much more to him than the latter. She had been devastated. Not so much by the loss of Jason, but by the defeat she was knowing all over again. Why was it so hard for people to love her? Her parents? Jason?

In college she'd dated, but always on a friendly basis, never with any promise of romance hovering on the horizon. As often as not her dates were with men who had asked Alicia out and been turned down because she was already busy. They'd turn to her roommate just to fill the empty night on their calendar. Her virginity hadn't been all that hard to hold onto. Few had bargained for it.

"What happened?"

She jumped slightly when Carter roused her out of her musings. "One day he just left, taking everything with him. He'd found someone better."

"I doubt that," he said tersely. When Sloan quickly looked at him, she was surprised to see that his bared teeth were clenched angrily. "Are you still . . . still . . ."

Soundlessly she laughed and shook her head.

"In love with him? No. It would never have worked. He'd have discovered someone more exciting—"

"Why in the hell do you persist in saying things like that?"

He fired the question at her with such impetus, she broke off what she'd been saying. He was truly angry, and that amazed her. He was leaning across the small table like a well-trained hound, ready to pounce on her if she made another wrong move.

"Have you looked in a mirror lately? Don't you know that you have four stunning colors of blond and brown in your hair and possibly a dozen or so more? A man would have to be crazy not to want to catalogue each one. Your eyes are haunting and rare in color and I'd have to work like hell to find the right words to describe them in a book. They have the darkest, longest lashes surrounding them that any woman could want. And your figure is luscious, though your wardrobe could stand some help. You try to hide that delectable body with frumpy clothes. That's what's wrong with you. You try to hide from yourself and everyone else. Why, dammit? Why?"

Pale and feeling abused by his verbal onslaught, she stared at him wordlessly. When he realized the wounding effect his attack had had on her, his tense posture relaxed and he fell back against the wrought iron chair. A blistering expletive soughed through his lips. After what seemed like a long while, he said softly, "You can kick me in the shins if you want to. Or better yet, step on my foot again. That still hurts like hell."

He succeeded in taking the anguish out of her eyes and bringing a smile to her chalky lips. "You should have lit into me now like you did this morning, Sloan. You don't let yourself go often enough. Give vent to your emotions, for godsakes."

"I'll try harder," she said. "Maybe you can give

me temper tantrum lessons during the month you're here."

"Any time you say." He was grinning, but they'd both been reminded that they were only on the second day into the month he'd be under her roof. Both were wondering how they were going to survive it and what they would tell Alicia if they were forced to call it off in order to retain their loyalty to her.

"You didn't finish your sundae," she observed quietly to break the spell of contemplative silence.

"I guess I got my fill of ice cream a few days ago. I took the boys out while Alicia was shopping. We had hot dogs and Adam got mustard on his shirt. Then the portion of David's ice cream that didn't get in his mouth, ended up in his lap or dripping off his sleeve. When we got home Alicia gave us all hell."

"I can understand why." Sloan joined his laughter, but it rang hollow. "Maybe you'll pick up some hints on keeping them clean after you're married."

"Yeah. Maybe." He was staring bleakly into the milky slush at the bottom of his sundae glass.

Sloan looked out the wide windows next to their table. It had begun to rain.

"Are your books autobiographical, Mr. Madison, or purely fiction?"

Carter set down his wine glass and surreptitiously winked at Sloan. "Miss Lehman, if everything I write about had happened to me, I doubt I'd have lived this long."

The others at the table laughed congenially.

The crab au gratin had turned out to be delicious. With the casserole she served a endive salad, asparagus garnished with lemon slices, and orange sherbet for dessert. She had begun her dinner preparations as soon as she and Carter returned to Fairchild House. He had gone upstairs, but, much as she had listened, Sloan didn't hear the tapping keys of his typewriter all afternoon.

She took time out to shower before serving dinner, dressing in a soft black wool skirt and white georgette blouse with a pleated bodice and pearl buttons on the left shoulder. Repeatedly she told herself that it was no softer and no more feminine a costume than she usually wore. She was proved wrong when two of the guests exclaimed over how pretty she looked when she called them from the parlor, where they had gathered for pre-dinner wine or cocktails, into the candlelit dining room. She blushed at their compliments, thanked them shyly, and refused to meet Carter's eyes.

He had come down to dinner wearing a navy sport coat over an open throated shirt of ivory silk, and gray slacks. For once it looked as though he'd made an attempt to control his thick mahogany hair, but the effort was just short of having been wasted. As Sloan served the first course, she studied him covertly. His hair wasn't curly, but swerved and dipped and clung to his scalp with a will of its own. It had decided a long time ago which way it wanted to grow around that well-shaped head and would forever defy blow dryers and stiff bristled brushes that tried to change its mind.

It was touchable hair, Sloan thought as she leaned over him to serve his salad. His scent rose from the V of his collar to caress her nostrils. He smelled clean and masculine, in a way that made her think of damp naked skin fresh from a shower. Her hand was trembling when she placed the salad plate in front of him. His eyes followed her slender hand back over his shoulder to meet her eyes. When he said, "Thank you, Ms. Fairchild," he could have been saying, "I've thought of how you look naked, too," and it couldn't have sounded more intimate.

Upon seeing him, one of the retired schoolteachers had splayed a veined hand over her meager breast and cried, "Carter Madison! I saw you on the *Today* show once. Oh, my goodness, I can't believe this. I've read all your books."

Indeed, she had one in her room which was rapidly fetched for him to autograph. The other guests were equally impressed to have a celebrity in their midst. It was the schoolteacher who had asked Carter about the autobiographical aspects of his writing in a breathy voice much more suited to a girl forty years the lady's junior.

He handled their curiosity and hero worship with aplomb and self-deprecation, which delighted them all. He regaled them with stories about his research, which had taken him virtually all over the world.

Sloan continued to serve the dinner with the same efficient deference she always did. Even though his voice never altered, she knew each time she entered the room from the kitchen, Carter's eyes followed her as she went about her tasks.

"Would everyone like coffee and brandy in the parlor by the fire?" Sloan asked graciously when they were finished eating. Everyone enthusiastically agreed. "I'll bring a tray in there. Make yourselves comfortable."

She went into the kitchen to make certain she hadn't forgotten anything on the tray. The door swung open behind her. Carter was carrying in one of the trays she used for serving dinner, heaped with dirty dishes.

"Carter!" she exclaimed. "What are you doing?"

He set the tray on the countertop. "Helping out a little."

"Well don't."

"Why?"

"*Why?* Because you're a guest. What would everyone think?"

The lines around his mouth tightened and he put his hands on his hips. "I don't give a damn what they think."

"Well I do. I have to."

"Since when is it a crime for a man to carry a heavy tray for a lady? Answer me that."

"You wouldn't bus your own table at a restaurant, would you?"

"Oh for . . ." He muttered an explicit curse his heroes were fond of using. "I'm tired, really tired of this servant scene you play out. It galls the hell out of me and makes me damn near as skittish as you are. It's fine for everyone else," he jerked his head in the general direction of the parlor, "but I don't expect it. They're only customers."

"And so are you," she lashed out. Her breasts were trembling beneath the sheerest, most elegant set of lingerie she owned. She had treated herself to wearing it tonight, and she wished to God now she hadn't. Carter's eyes were searing through her blouse as though to burn it away and find the cause of the agitation so visibly stirring the fabric.

"You have beautiful breasts. They're trembling. Why, Sloan?"

"Oh." Folding her arms across her chest protectively, she groped through the chaos of her mind for the end of the slipping rope of her composure. "Don't say things like that to me. I'll have to ask you to leave Fairchild House just as I would any male guest who said . . ."

"Guest! That's self-defensive crap. What about a *man?* What about a man telling a woman he wants more with each passing hour that she has beautiful—"

"I said stop it or you'll have to leave!" She couldn't meet the fury in his eyes, so she turned her back, keeping her posture rigid. "You're a customer in my place of business. That's all you are, Carter," she said to the floor. "A customer."

He muttered an obscenity more colorful than the last as he shoved through the door on his angry exit.

It was several minutes before Sloan could calm herself enough to heft the heavy tray and carry it into the parlor. She knew what she'd said about asking him to leave had been an empty threat, but she hoped Carter wouldn't think so. They were treading in treacherous water that threatened to drag them both below the surface. This talking at love, their visual insinuations and invitations, were flirting disaster for everyone concerned. For her, for Carter, for Alicia and her boys. It had been necessary to tell Carter exactly where he stood. He had to be made to feel he was nothing special. *He isn't*, she averred as she went down the hallway.

Of one thing she was sure. Tonight, as soon as she took it off, her best set of lingerie was going back in the drawer and it would be a long time before she wore it again. It made her feel far too feminine, far too vulnerable, and too ludicrously close to tears.

He was kneeling in front of the fireplace when she entered, adding logs to the bright fire she'd laid before her shower and lit while the guests were eating dinner. "Mr. Madison," she said with a tight smile, "you shouldn't have bothered." This was for the benefit of the other four guests who were ensconced in the comfortable easy chairs and sofas Sloan had procured and upholstered herself.

"No trouble, Ms. Fairchild. You've made me feel so at home, I didn't even think about it." His words were dripping with sarcasm that apparently only she was privy to. The others were nodding their heads as though he were an oracle spouting gems of wisdom.

She left them, offering to replenish the china coffee pot if they should need more. In between bites of her own dinner kept warm in the oven, she stacked the dishes in the industrial-sized dishwasher and put the dining room back in order, setting it for breakfast. She squeezed fresh oranges into a sealable plastic container and stored the juice in the refrigerator to be served from a crystal pitcher the next morning. She whipped butter with honey and made the batter for tomorrow's pancakes, again storing it in the refrigerator.

She plastered on a smile before returning to the parlor, but was relieved to find the room empty. Taking up the large tray, she returned it to the kitchen. She checked the fireplace one last time, making sure the firescreen was in place and that the fire was burning down safely. The doors were secured and the lights turned off before she went to her room.

She was down to her slip when she heard the faint tap on her door. That was a first. No one had ever sought her out in her room. A guest, if one should need her, was to press the small button on the light switch in his room, and a buzzer would sound in her room, in the kitchen, and in her office.

"Yes? Who is it?" It was superfluous to ask. She knew who it was.

"Me."

She pressed her fingertips to her lips. "Go away, Carter."

"I have to talk to you."

"You can't come in my room!" she cried softly. "Please go away before someone sees or hears you."

"Then meet me in the parlor." He paused before adding. "I'll come back if you're not there in five minutes."

It took her that long to stop shaking. She knew it was foolhardy to respond to his summons, but she was more than a little afraid that he'd carry out his threat if she didn't. Tightly belting the same dowdy robe she'd had on the night before and slipping into a pair of scuffs, she cautiously opened her door and moved silently through the darkened house toward the parlor. As soon as she entered the room, Carter stepped out of the shadows, walked her backward, and pinned her against the wall with his body.

"Sloan, Sloan," he groaned into her hair, nuzzling it with his mouth and nose.

"No, Carter." The firelight had just enough remnant life to dance on his hair, burnishing the deep russet strands to copper. She longed to plow through the mass and hold his head fast against her neck where his face had burrowed.

She forfeited her chance. His head came up suddenly, fiercely, and it was his hands that threaded through her hair, holding her head still as he peered into the swirling pools of her eyes.

"I've been a good little boy all day. I've done not one damn thing I have to be ashamed of. I've sat at that bitch of a typewriter all afternoon trying to come up with a sentence that has a subject and verb and makes some kind of sense, and I'll be damned if I could. I've not had one idea that didn't involve you—"

"No—"

"Yes!" he said on a hissing whisper. His breath was fragrant. He'd imbibed more brandy than coffee. Maybe that's why his face was hot and flushed. Or did the brandy have anything to do with it? He ground his hips against her as he moved closer and she closed her eyes and moaned her own sweet agony. "I've thought of nothing but you since you opened the door last night. I've done nothing but imagine having you beneath me, loving me."

"Stop," she begged. "Don't say anymore. Please. For everyone's sake. Carter, *think*. Think of Alicia and David and Adam. They're depending on your love. They need you."

"And I need you," he said, crushing her against him and placing his mouth against her ear where he repeated, "I need *you*."

Her teeth drew blood when they sank into her bottom lip. Tears eked out from underneath eyes squeezed shut. How she overcame the need to surrender to what they both wanted, she didn't know, but somehow she willed herself to push away from him. "You can't have me," she said on heaving breaths, still keeping him at a distance with stiff arms. "You know that. I know it. So please don't do this to me again."

Then she was fleeing down the hallway to the sterile, frigid safety of her room.

He took his meals with the others in the dining room. Otherwise she didn't see him for the next few days. She waited until she knew he had gone out before she changed the linens on his bed and supplied his bathroom with fresh towels. On such visits to the room he occupied, she tried not to look at his personal items, his shaving things on the shelf over the basin in the bathroom, his clothes draped over various pieces of furniture. One day she indulged herself and hung the discarded garments in the closet. Ostensibly she was straightening the room, when all she was really doing was providing herself with an excuse to touch something belonging to him, something he'd touched.

He was polite, but aloof. When the banker and his wife and the two schoolteachers left, they were replaced by two couples traveling together from Iowa. He was immediately recognized and recounted the same entertaining stories for this audience, if not as expansively as before. In the evenings, he either excused himself and went to his room, or left Fairchild House entirely, returning several hours later.

He received a letter from David, if the broadly printed scrawl on the envelope were any indication of the sender. Sloan left it at his place setting at dinner.

"Thank you, Ms. Fairchild," he said, holding up the letter.

"You're welcome, Mr. Madison."

One day a man identifying himself as Carter's agent called and asked to speak to him. Trepidatiously Sloan climbed the stairs and knocked on the door. The pounding typewriter keys stopped abruptly.

"What is it?" His tone would have made the warning hiss of an angry rattler sound convivial.

"Your agent is calling long distance. Do you want to talk to him?"

"No."

The typewriting started again and Sloan politely reported his curt message to the aggravated agent.

"Mr. Madison," she called from the kitchen one afternoon when she heard his heavy tread coming through the front door. He was poised on the stairs looking down at her when she caught up with him. She'd been ironing the mountain of napkins and tablecloths, sheets and pillowcases that accumulated on an exhaustively regular basis. It was too expensive to send them out. The heat from the iron had brought a spot of color to both cheeks. Her hair had been piled on top of her head, but a boiling cauldron of spaghetti to be used in tetrazzini had caused several strands to fall in humid curls around her face and on her neck. She had no idea how domestically fetching she was as she looked up at him. "Alicia called. She wants you to call her back."

He loped down the stairs. "Anything wrong?"

"No," she said breathlessly. This was the first time she had allowed herself to meet his eyes in days. He was windblown and smelled wonderfully of rain. It glistened on his hair and the shoulders of his jacket. Where had he been? she wondered. "I don't think so. You can use the phone in my office."

She led him to the tiny cubicle and then turned away.

"You can stay."

"I'm sure you and your fiancée have private things to say to each other." Sloan felt sorry for the telephone as he grabbed the receiver and punched the digits of Alicia's number with a vengeance.

She had carried a stack of fresh sheets upstairs to a linen closet and was on her way down when she met him coming up the stairs. "Did you get through?"

"Yes. She asked me how my book was coming."

"How *is* it coming?"

"It's a pile of garbage," he growled as he proceeded up the stairs without slowing his tread.

Sloan put on a good act, never giving her other guests a hint of the tension and turmoil inside. But every night when she went to her room, she would curl into a tight ball beneath her covers and try to still the fluttering demands of her body. Every inch of flesh seemed to scream for Carter's touch.

She couldn't forget how inescapably he'd held her, yet how gentle his hands were. Too well she remembered how his eyes had toured her the day he held her on the bed. His breath had been hot and urgent on her skin the night he'd whispered, "I need you," in her ear. Speaking it aloud had been unnecessary. She could feel his need, hard and insistent, against her supple, receptive body.

She went through her days mechanically, preparing the meals with no less competence, but perhaps a little less pleasure, It was with that kind of automation that she was clearing the kitchen late one night a week after the scene in the parlor. All the guests had gone upstairs long ago, so she turned in startled reaction when she heard the noise behind her.

Carter was standing just within the door. "I didn't mean to scare you."

"I . . . I thought you were upstairs." He'd taken off the sport coat he always wore at dinner. The tails of his shirt were hanging around his hips and it was only half-buttoned as though he'd just put it on out of necessity.

"I was. I have a blasted headache and don't have anything to take for it. I wondered if you might have an aspirin. Something?"

"Yes, yes, of course." She despised the flustered, rushed, breathless sound of her voice. Why couldn't she sound cool, but concerned, and get him the damn aspirin without going to jelly in the process? "In my bathroom."

She was back in less than a minute bearing several bottles of over-the-counter analgesics. "You must get a helluva lot of headaches." The eyebrow she adored arched in humor.

"I didn't know which you'd prefer. Some upset the stomach." God, she sounded like one of those ninnies in the commercials.

"This ought to do." He selected a bottle of plain aspirin and shook two out in his hand. "Water?"

She dashed to the cabinet and took down a glass her guests never saw. It had Bugs Bunny and Elmer Fudd on it. His brow curved again when she handed it to him, sloshing tap water over her shaky hand in the process. He tossed down the two aspirins and took a long drink.

"Thank you," he said, setting the glass down.

"I hope it works on your headache."

"Aren't you up late?"

"I made a gelatin mold. I had to chop up a lot of . . . stuff."

"Oh. All done?"

"Yes, I was just putting things away."

"Do these go up there?" he asked, referring to

two heavy mixing bowls and the third shelf of an opened cabinet.

"Yes." She reached for the bowls, but he stepped around her and picked them up.

"You'll pull a muscle in your back," he said, easily placing the bowls on the high shelf. "You need a step stool or something."

"I guess so."

"Sloan." He spun around to face her and all the placid indifference, the polite inconsequentials, had deserted him. He took her shoulders beneath his hands. "Sloan," he repeated in a more mellow tone as his eyes wandered hungrily over her face, "we've got a serious problem going on here."

"Serious problem?" Her voice was high and airy.

"Yes."

"With your room? Your headache? The—"

"You don't know what our problem is?" The low, velvety voice stroked the inside of her thighs and made them warm.

Tears clouded her eyes. Her lips began to tremble. She shook her head in remorse. "No."

"Yes, you do," he countered. Then his lips closed firm and warm over hers.

Chapter Four

Her only resistance was a momentary tension in her muscles when his arms went around her and anchored her against him. A small cry of astonishment was trapped by his lips as they opened over hers. They were fanatical in their lust to possess, acting solely out of hunger, carnal and beyond control.

Stunned, Sloan gripped his biceps for balance. As his hands scoured her back, she felt the wonder of his hard muscles bunching and stretching. The feel of them moving with sleek precision in her palms was marvelous and she softly moaned her approval.

"Sloan." Her name became his love-chant as he pressed her face into the warm hollow of his neck. His arms enfolded her as securely and warmly as a fur lined cape. He adjusted his body to hers, instructing her with stroking hands how to mold herself to him in a perfect, breathtaking fit. He held her there for a seemingly endless time, while their hearts pulsed together and chronicled their mounting passion.

Then he lifted her face to his and captured her lips with tethered violence. Their heads rolled from side to side, twisting their lips together, bumping their noses, seeking an outlet for the energy that zephyred through them. Suddenly he was impatient with the fury of it and fused his mouth with hers to still them. A bold thrust of his tongue broke the barrier of her lips and teeth.

A deep growl rumbled in his chest as he swept her mouth with a marauding tongue intent on conquest. He plundered her sweetly, delving deeply into the farthest recess of the honeyed cove, taking up every part of it and making it his. He stroked her mouth, rapidly, slowly, mercilessly, persuasively. The tip of his tongue rubbed against hers in a challenge to join the skirmish. To his delight she did.

Her tongue darted out to bathe his lips with the taste of her. He caught her lower lip between his teeth in a gentle bite. She sipped at his lips, flirtatiously and elusively, until his tongue sank once again into the luscious temptation of her mouth. He made love to it. First with light quick thrusts, then with stronger, slower, deeper ones.

Sloan lost all track of time, of space and distance, of right and wrong. She had wanted this. From the instant she saw him standing on the doorstep, she had wanted his lips on hers, his hands moving over her body as they were now with an audacious curiosity that wouldn't be denied. His whispered love words and moans of gratification were the music she had wanted to hear falling on her ears. Tentacles of desire ribboned through her, choking off every remnant of conscience.

She was powerless to stop or resist this tidal wave of passion. It had been inevitable and irreversible, gaining momentum since the instant they first saw each other. Impossible to outrun, to withstand, she could only let it wash over her now and flood her with its magic. Her whole body was left renewed, cleansed of loneliness, wealthy with desire.

A shuddering sigh tripped through her lips when his hands slid around from her back to the blades of her hipbones. Each thumb found the crest of one and rotated hypnotically while his fingers curled around her hips to hold her fast. He dipped his knees slightly until he could nestle hard and throbbing in the cradle of her femininity. He rubbed against her in measured circles, moving with a grinding motion that spread a flushing heat from there into her chest. She was melting, flowering, moistening in expectation.

"Carter, Carter," she sobbed, clutching at his hair with frantic hands. In her head a thousand bells were peeling joyously and her heart was bursting with love. Yes, love! She loved him, and the lips that were worshipping her throat with ardent kisses told her he felt the same. "I can't believe this."

"I know, my love, I know. God, it's wonderful. I knew it would be."

He sought the buttons of her blouse and undid them deftly. Then he pulled back to look at her as he parted the garment. Her brassiere was of a sheer, glossy flesh-colored fabric that encased her like a second skin designed to entice. Virginally pink nipples were pouting seductively, thrusting rebelliously against their confinement. He answered their request and brushed his fingers across them with the softest of caresses.

"Please," she begged in a ragged voice. "Touch me, touch me."

"You're beautiful."

He cupped a breast in each palm and lifted her slightly. He found the ripe peaks daintier and sweeter than in his fantasy, but no less responsive as his thumbs rolled over them repeatedly until they were hard with yearning. He lay his cheek against the plump curve of her and snuggled. His breath touched her first, warm and damp, then his tongue nudged her nipple through the gossamer brassiere cup. Again. Then again, while she was breathing in harsh and rapid pants.

When his lips closed around her and drew her inside his mouth, she arched against him reflexively. She tore at the buttons of his shirt and when they were opened, combed through the thick mat of hair on his chest. His own sighs of unrestrained pleasure harmonized with hers as his mouth continued its sweet foreplay.

Her fingers engaged in an orgy of new sensations, detailing each masculine aspect of his chest. The firm contours of the muscles, the rippling track of ribs, the hard flat nipples were all examined with hedonistic fingers. The crinkly hair thinned and softened beneath hands that grew braver and moved lower.

He nuzzled the cleavage between her breasts and breathed deeply of her scent. "Sloan," he murmured. He caught one of her hands and, moving slowly, giving her time to object if she should be so cruel, lowered it and pressed it against the fullness in his trousers.

"From wanting you, Sloan. From wanting to be inside you."

His mouth came back to hers and this time the ferocity was replaced with finesse. His tongue swirled inside her mouth until she was dizzy with her need of him. One hand remained on her breast, his fingers squeezing in a gentle milking motion. The other hand glided past the waistband of her skirt, down, down, to close tenderly over the mound of her womanhood.

"May God forgive me," she whimpered. "I want you too."

He moved but slightly, yet she could feel electric

currents from each of his fingers shooting into her, igniting a million cells with a burning desire to know all of that which surged with life in her hand. His hand moved again, sliding between her thighs. She convulsed against it and whispered his name in a tormented litany.

He shuddered like one palsied before his hands fell away from the treasures of her body and he took several stumbling steps backward. "Dammit," he cursed before several more colorful expletives were pushed through his teeth. When he saw her ravaged expression, he came to her quickly and took her face between his hands. "I'm sorry, Sloan, to stop like that, but I just can't do it."

She clamped both hands over her mouth to stopper a cry of mortification. She tried to escape him, and when he would have detained her, she fought savagely, whirling away from him. "Don't touch me again," she ground out, when he reached for her. Her outstretched hands staved off his advances. "Leave me alone."

He was dumbfounded by her reaction. "Sloan, I—"

"No need for explanations. If you hadn't stopped us, I would have," she said, grappling with the buttons of her blouse that refused to cooperate. "You're absolutely right. We can't do it. I don't know what happened to me, I . . ." Her voice trailed off and she pressed her fingers into her temples that seemed about to explode with the blood still pounding through them. "You . . . Alicia . . . I should never have kissed you."

"What the hell are you talking about?" he asked in supreme frustration. "My calling a halt to things had nothing to do with Alicia."

Through vague, bewildered, dilated eyes, she stared at him uncomprehendingly.

"I couldn't go through with it because of my fantasy, because of my own warped imagination."

"What? Fantasy?"

"Oh, hell." He dropped into a chair at the table and buried his face in his hands. For several seconds he held that dejected pose while Sloan stood motionless and stared at him. She wished she would petrify there, that she'd never be required to make a decision, that she'd never have to move from that spot, that she would forevermore be emotionally dead.

At last he raised his head and said wearily, "Sit down, Sloan, so we can talk."

"No. I don't—"

"Don't argue with me for once," he barked. "Just sit down and listen." After a short pause he added a terse, "Please."

She took the chair across the table from him and sat with prim rigidity, almost as a punishment for the wanton woman she'd been minutes earlier.

"The morning after I arrived here, I was daydreaming up in my room," he began. "It's silly, I know, but as a writer I spend a great deal of my time daydreaming, envisioning things to happen to my characters. Anyway, *I* was the character this time and I saw us together, in this room, doing what we were just about to do."

She swallowed and continued to stare at her hands that were knotted together, white and cold, on the edge of the table.

He grinned shyly. "It was a terrific daydream, but somehow I couldn't apply it to real life. When I make love to you the first time, I don't want it to be furtive and rushed. I want us to be naked and at leisure and able to enjoy each other. I don't want our loving to be cheapened."

She was shaking her head. "No, Carter. Don't talk about . . . about that. It must never happen under any conditions."

"Sloan, am I wrong?" he asked in a pained voice. "Don't you love me?"

She raised her head to meet his anxious eyes

with hers, which were swimming with tears. Two escaped and trekked down her cheeks as she nodded, at first hesitantly, then more insistently. "Yes, yes, yes."

He seemed vastly, endearingly relieved as he released his breath on a great whoosh and reached for her hand. He examined it as it lay listlessly in his. "Every time I've come near you, I've behaved like a sex maniac. I've backed you into walls, tossed you down on a bed and held you there. I didn't plan on anything happening when I came downstairs tonight. I didn't contrive a headache just to catch you alone and force you against the kitchen countertop. I swear to God I didn't."

"You didn't force me to do anything."

He smiled again and let his eyes range over her face and mussed hair. "I'm a man, Sloan. I've been turned down, as any guy honest enough to admit it has. But I've also had more than my share of women all over the world. I've taken them heartlessly and quickly for my own satisfaction. Rarely did I care if I ever saw them again." He gripped her hand tight. "That's not what it is this time. This is not only lust. Believe that. I don't want you to think that I consider you a convenient body that's good for a few rolls in the hay while I'm under your roof as if you went with the rent."

She blushed and glanced away. "I didn't think that. How do you know I'm not a landlady who would like that sort of temporary set-up with a virile tenant?"

His eyes wrinkled at the corners when he smiled. "Because you're rare and fine. Because you can still blush when I say something just this side of dirty."

They laughed together and it was a rich sound, filling the corners of the still room and encapsulating them in their private world.

"I've had a helluva time writing this past week," he admitted. "I've been writing about something for years when I didn't know a damn thing about it. And the worst of it is, I didn't even know I didn't know."

He pushed up from the table and went to stand at the sink, staring at the rain that dripped monotonously from the eaves. "In each of my books I had a love interest, sometimes a triangle, but always some form of romance. I convinced myself and tried to convince my readers that my hero was always in love with the girl. Now I know I was writing *at* love without ever having known what it felt like."

He turned back to her. "Now that I know, now that I've met you, I'm dissatisfied with everything I've written because it doesn't convey the total absorption a man has with a woman when he loves her. I want to express that sense of helplessness with this book. Gregory really loves this girl and it's going to kill him to have to . . . to . . ."

"To leave her," she finished numbly.

"I'm not going to think about that," Carter said angrily.

Sloan came to her feet. "We have to, Carter. You're engaged to my best friend, the only person in the world who has ever cared about me. We love each other as friends. I came so close tonight to betraying that friendship and I can't risk it again. She's my *friend*."

"Dammit, she's my friend too," he shouted, and when she looked nervously toward the ceiling, he repeated it on a emphatic whisper. "She's my friend, too. And that's the way I love her, Sloan."

She covered her ears. "No. You shouldn't tell me this."

He strode toward her and removed her hands. "Maybe not, but you're going to hear it. I think Alicia's a great lady, a little flighty and irresponsible, but charmingly so. She was Jim's wife and she made my best friend happy. That was reason enough to love her.

"But I asked her to marry me because it was convenient to both of us, Sloan. She and the boys need a keeper. I felt duty bound to Jim to take care of them. The time has come in my life when I should have a wife and children. That's the only reason I asked her to marry me. I know she's still in love with Jim and I've never entertained any romantic notions about her."

She pulled free of his restraining hands and turned away. "But you'll . . . you'll sleep with her once you're married."

He took a long time to answer while the pieces of her breaking heart fell to the bottom of her soul one by one. "I would like at least one child of my own," he said softly at last. "When I do marry, I have every intention of sleeping with my wife every night."

Sloan's eyes slammed shut and she wished she could close off her ears just as effectively. "Yes, of course you will. It was stupid of me to ask."

"But Alicia might not be my wife."

She jerked around quickly. "Of course she'll be your wife."

He stubbornly refused to concede it. "Not necessarily."

"Yes, necessarily."

"How can you say that after what has happened between us, Sloan? How can you even think I could marry Alicia now?"

"And how can you think otherwise?" she demanded heatedly. "Carter, she trusted me enough to send you here. To place you in my keeping."

"That was foolish of her."

She wouldn't accept his compliment. "No it wasn't. She has every reason to trust me with the man she plans to marry. We're friends and neither of us has ever betrayed that friendship. What if the situation were reversed? What if Alicia had died and I was engaged to Jim? Could you take me away from him?"

He broadened her vocabulary with a few words she'd never heard spoken aloud. "It's not the same."

"It's exactly the same. And you know it. Don't you see, Carter? It's only because we're living in the same house. We've been forced together and we've let our imaginations run wild. You naturally have a romantic nature to be able to write the way you do. You're only letting it work overtime. I'm lonely, having lived alone for years. Once you get back to Alicia and the boys—"

"That's crap, Sloan. Now you're the one being less than honest. Don't you think I'm man enough to know what I want? I could have found you in a supermarket as you bumped into my cart or in an elevator or anywhere and I'd have known you with the same familiarity as I did the other night when you opened your door to me."

"Alicia will be a wonderful wife," she said desperately, twisting her hands. She loved the words pouring out of his mouth, but knew she shouldn't be listening to them, much less cherishing each one.

"No doubt she will, but will she be wonderful for me? She doesn't respect my need for solitude when I'm working. If she were here, she'd be running up those stairs knocking on the door every ten minutes—"

"Stop!"

"No. You listen," He gripped her shoulders and shook her slightly until her head wobbled back and she was forced to heed his words. "Would I be good for her? I suffer every writer's paranoia, Sloan. I need to talk. To converse. Often. And to someone who will listen. I mean *really* listen. You do. Like the other night when I arrived, you sat at that table and listened. I had your undivided attention. You weren't bubbling over to relate to me everything that had happened to you during the day. You weren't up and down like a damn jack-in-the-box—"

"Damn you, Carter!" She yanked herself free and backed away from him. "Don't you dare stand there and criticize the woman you're going to marry to me. That's what men do when they pick up a woman in a bar, gain her sympathy so she'll have sex with them. 'My wife doesn't understand me.' Brilliant as you are, can't you come up with something more original than that? I don't want to hear it. It makes me feel dirty.

"If you and Alicia have problems that need ironing out, then iron them out privately. I don't want to know about them or be involved in them."

"Well that's too damn bad because you *are* involved, Sloan." He drew her to him again and, though she struggled, he wouldn't release her. "From the top of your beautiful head to the tips of your ten toes and at all points in between, you're involved." He sealed her mouth to his with a sweet suction. One hand held her jaw imprisoned while a reckless tongue plundered her mouth. The other hand curved over her hip, pressing her close, acquainting her once again with the power of his desire.

With every ounce of depleting moral fiber, she fought the erotic impulses rioting through her. But to no avail. She'd been dead too long. When offered new life, she couldn't refuse the resurrection. He felt her acquiescence, gradually relaxed his hold, and let his hand slip between them to fondle her breasts with a loving caress. Through her restored clothing, his knuckles feathered over the nipples that had already budded with desire.

"If anyone has my child, I want it to be you, Sloan. I want a baby of mine to nurse on your sweet, sweet breasts."

The verbal picture he painted was right out of her dreams. A man who loved her. A baby their mutual love had created. A sense of belonging. A sense of worth. Being loved in return.

But she knew, as with all her dreams, this one would never come true. His kisses, his caresses were only making her crave something she could never have. Loving him was a masochistic self-flagellation that left her heart lacerated and bleeding. He would come to his senses and return to Alicia and Sloan would be left alone with her wounds. She wasn't sure she could heal herself again.

He was so wrapped up in their kiss, that he blinked stupidly and incredulously when she pushed him away. "Don't say things like that to me." Her face was a hard cold mask that if she didn't guard carefully would crumple. "Don't approach me like this again or I'll have to ask you to leave Fairchild House."

Smoldering rage burned away the passion-induced fog in his eyes. They were suddenly brilliant with clarity. "Dammit, Sloan—"

"I mean it. You're going to marry someone else. Kindly remember that."

His sizzling opinion of her reminder was branded into the ceiling and she cringed at the blunt vulgarity. "I know what's wrong with you," he said with a feral curl to his lip. "You've imprisoned yourself in this house, hidden yourself from the world because you're afraid to face it."

"Afraid?" she asked, insulted and not a little in fear of his uncanny talent to strip her of defenses and see into her innermost, secret self.

"Yes, afraid. You grew up in a house that sounds about as cheerful as a dusty mausoleum. Your parents, from the bits and pieces I've picked up from you and Alicia, ignored you. In what I think was sheer desperation, you latched onto a jackass of a boyfriend who dumped you."

"Shut up. You don't know anything about it."

"The hell I don't. You may think you're hiding,

but you give yourself away, Sloan. You're as transparent as glass. So what if your parents were inept? So what if an egomaniacal bastard went fickle on you? Is that any reason to draw a circle around yourself and not let another human being inside it for the rest of your life?"

"Go to hell," she said, spinning away from him.

Undaunted by her flair of spirit, he lunged after her, catching her just before she could retreat into her room. He braced her against him and held her fast. "You've doomed yourself to a life of loneliness because you're under the misguided notion that that's all you deserve. Hell, Sloan, none of us get what we deserve or we'd never even be born. Life doesn't depend on merit or we'd all be angels . . . or devils."

"Let me go." Futilely she struggled for release.

"You've thrown yourself upon the sacrificial altar of self-denial and are afraid of letting anyone, especially a man, touch you. This god of martyrdom you've dedicated yourself to is jealous and might not like a sacrifice sullied by happiness and love."

He was so close to the truth that she clawed back like a wild animal. Tossing back her hair, she glared up at him. "What about you, Carter? You're just the opposite. You've dedicated yourself to a woman and two children who need you, yet you'd toss that promise aside as though it never existed. But it does exist and it is binding and before too long you'll remember that. You'll think about Jim and what you feel is your duty toward him as a friend. You'll go back to Alicia and the boys and give them all the love you so blithely extol to me. No thanks. You'll eventually come to your senses and in the meantime, I won't be your playmate." Her body was tautly drawn up as she gulped at precious air. "I think it would be best if you left here."

He was fairly bristling with temper and his eyes

blazed hotly. He flung his arms wide when he released her, as though touching her an instant longer was loathsome. With lips that barely moved, he strained his parting words out. "Your bed will remain sacrosanct, Ms. Fairchild, but you'll not kick me out of here."

The swinging door oscillated back and forth several times after he shoved his way through it. Finally it came to a standstill. Only then did Sloan realize how exhausted she was. She groped her way into her room and collapsed on her bed, drawing her pillow close and burying her face into it.

His perceptive accusations had left her feeling beaten and battered. Her soul had been his target and each angry outburst a missile aimed at it, striking her where it hurt the most. The truth of his words had been the ammunition in each attack.

Why couldn't Carter understand? *I have no recourse except to protect myself. I will not be hurt by love again!*

But she already did love again and was already hurt by it. No matter the scathing words she'd flung at him, she loved Carter with an intensity close to pain.

She hadn't been prepared for the heartache of Jason's rejection. She had entered into that relationship blindly and without the benefit of experience and warning. This time she would have no excuse for such naïvete. If she followed the path her heart was telling her to, the road would be paved with regret. It had a dead end. Better to turn back now while she still could.

But how was she going to cope with having him in her house? If he worked in his room during the days, she'd probably see him only in the evenings when he came to the dining room for dinner. She would carry no more trays up to him. If he didn't come down to breakfast, he wouldn't get any. Perhaps she'd survive the next few weeks. Perhaps.

It wasn't as though they'd be alone. There would be other people in the house.

The next day newspapers were filled with stories about the unusual amount of rain the Bay Area was having and the consequences of it.

Sloan hadn't really been concentrating on the inclement weather. Her mind had been too occupied elsewhere. On Carter. So she was mildly surprised to read about the mudslides reported in the hills surrounding the city and the local flooding in lower areas. The conditions became disastrous enough to make television network news for the next several days.

"Maybe we should cut our stay short and head for home," one of the women from Iowa said at dinner.

"Naw," her husband drawled. "We planned this trip for months. You won't let a little rain ruin it for us, will you?"

Worriedly, the lady turned to their traveling companions. "What do you think we should do?"

"Stay," the man said, spearing a piece of grilled steak from the platter Sloan held for him.

"I suppose so," the second woman said. "Besides, Dorothy," she teased. "It's not raining in any of the stores."

Both husbands groaned and Sloan sighed with relief. The only other guests she had in the house were an elderly couple who were only staying two more nights. She dared not look at Carter through the entire exchange, though she could feel his sardonic gaze on her.

"No question of my leaving," he said, taking a sip of burgundy wine. "I'm making terrific headway on my book. Oh, Ms. Fairchild, another helping of those potatoes, please," he said with a dazzling smile that only she knew was false.

"Certainly, Mr. Madison," she said with equally insincere graciousness and a demonic urge to dump the contents of his plate in his lap.

Keeping a wary eye on the weather, Sloan was dismayed to watch the situation worsen. The Golden Gate Bridge was closed to traffic for hours at a time because high winds and torrential rains made driving across it perilous.

Sloan began to panic. The couples from Iowa fulfilled their stay, but the elderly couple was due to leave the following day. She had two rooms reserved for the weekend, but she was afraid tourists would hear the discouraging weather reports, which the news reporters seemed bent on painting as black as possible, and cancel their trips. Not only would that severely affect her budget, but it would also mean she and Carter would be alone. Unless she could convince him to leave—and she thought the possibilities of that were about as good as those of the rain stopping any time soon.

Her worst fears came to fruition. Within an hour she got cancellation calls from both her weekend reservations. Despondently she sat at her desk in the cramped office under the stairs and ran tape after tape through the adding machine, praying the earlier tabulations would prove to be in error. How was she going to pay this month's bills? At least worrying over money kept her from worrying over Carter. By tomorrow night, they would be in the house alone.

It was with certain dread that she picked up the telephone when it rang later that day. "Fairchild House," she said with the resignation of one who knows it must be a creditor calling.

"You sound as dismal as the weather there is supposed to be."

"Alicia?" Her heart flopped over in her chest,

but she swore to herself it wasn't out of guilt. She'd only kissed him, for heaven's sake. Well, and sort of touched . . . "How are you?"

"Fine. The boys are fine. Nothing's wrong, I just wanted to call."

"I'll go get Carter. He's working as usual. I swear I rarely see him. He's locked up there in his room all the time. The typewriter is constantly clacking." *Easy, easy. Don't oversell it. She'll get suspicious.*

"Actually, Sloan, I wanted to talk to you," Alicia said quietly. "How does Carter seem to you?"

Sloan licked suddenly parched lips. "Seem?" She was twisting the telephone cord with rubbery fingers. "What do you mean?"

"Is he well? Happy?"

"Well? Happy?"

"Sloan, will you please stop repeating everything I say and tell me if he's all right?" Alicia said impatiently.

Sloan took several deep breaths. "Of course he's all right. Healthwise anyway. He packs away a good dinner every night." She hoped that shallow, affected laugh sounded sincere to Alicia. "I . . . I keep coffee on the stove for him. He . . . uh . . . he said he likes to drink it while he's working."

"At least he's eating. When he threatened to take a room at a hotel until the book was finished, I vetoed that. He'd live on potato chips and coffee out of a vending machine. I still think Fairchild House is the best thing for him right now, only . . ."

"Only?" Sloan squeaked when Alicia paused. Her heart was thudding against the back of her throat.

"Only he sounds funny when I talk to him. Distracted. Distant. I know he's working and he's always preoccupied, in another world, you know, when he's into a book, but I can't help but feel a little hurt by his lack of attention."

"I'm sure you're justified in feeling that way,

Alicia," Sloan said slowly. "Naturally you're wrapped up in wedding plans, but I think women put more stock in things like that than men do. He's terribly busy. I'm sure he's just concentrating on his book and his seeming indifference doesn't mean there's anything for you to worry about." A guilty conscience made the words taste brassy.

"I guess you're right," Alicia said on a brighter note. "I've got to get used to his 'dark periods' when he's brooding over a plot."

"Yes, you do." Sloan said seriously. "I've learned one thing about your fiancé. He takes his writing seriously."

"Well he should. He makes a bundle at it."

Sloan was unaccountably offended. She was sure Carter would write if he never made another penny from it, if he'd *never* made a penny from it.

". . . so I was thinking I might come up there tomorrow night and spend the weekend with the two of you."

Sloan was yanked back into the conversation in the middle of Alicia's speech. "What? Come up here? Tomorrow? That would be wonderful!" She meant it. Alicia's presence would set things right.

"Mother's offered to keep the boys. Do you have an extra bed?"

"Too many I'm afraid," Sloan said with a bitter laugh. "Please come."

"I've heard the weather is deplorable."

"So? We'll sit by the fire and visit while Carter's working."

"I'm hoping I can get him to take the weekend off."

"Let me go get Carter. I'm sure—"

"No. You can tell him I'm coming. If I'm going to disrupt his whole weekend, I'll leave him in peace today."

She told Sloan her tentative travel arrangements and estimated time of arrival, saying she'd get a cab from the airport and save her or Carter from getting out. "I'd rather you be there waiting for me with one of your scrumptious meals."

"You've got it. I can't wait to see you."

"Me, too. 'Bye."

Sloan felt like she'd been granted a reprieve. She approached the dinner hour with more enthusiasm than she'd known in days. Her spirit flagged somewhat when only the elderly couple came to the dining room.

"We met the other gentleman on the stairs and he said to tell you he was going out," the man said politely.

"Oh. Thank you."

He didn't come in until after midnight. She was sitting in the parlor waiting for him. He shrugged out of his coat and was shaking the rain off it when he looked up and saw her under the archway.

"What are you, the housemother? Didn't I make the curfew?"

Her lips compressed with anger and her back went as straight as a crowbar. "I don't care what time you come in, Mr. Madison. I waited up to give you a message from your fiancée."

The insolent slant of his lips fell and his shoulders slumped. He stared at his rain-splattered shoes. "I'm sorry, Sloan. I'm acting like a class-A bastard. I apologize."

His smug taunting was almost easier to take than this abject apology. He looked vulnerable and in need of comforting, standing there forlornly with rain dripping from his clothes. She supposed it was small compensation that he looked as miserable as she herself had been, but it only made her love him more.

His eyes were haunted and his voice empty when he asked, "Is everything all right? The boys?"

"Yes, everyone is fine. She's coming up tomorrow evening to spend the weekend with . . . you." She had started to say "us." But putting it this way made it sound more personal and solidified the relationship between him and Alicia.

"Ah," he nodded, his face expressionless. "That's good. Alone?" He forced interest into the question.

"David and Adam are staying with Alicia's parents. She'll be here in time for dinner."

For the first time in days they were alone. And while each was remembering moments of passion and anger, they wanted to squeeze as much time as possible out of this mundane conversation.

He couldn't help but notice that she wasn't wearing the ugly blue robe. This one was apricot-colored velour. The color highlighted the varying shades of gold and brown in her hair and the fabric molded over the shapely curves of her breasts and hips to fall softly between her legs. It was all he could do to keep his eyes off that delicate triangle so provocatively outlined.

There was nothing he could do about the congestion in his loins, but he cleared his throat against its own tightening constriction. "Did she say anything else?"

Her eyes homed in on the pulse beating at the base of his throat and stared at it, wishing she could feel its rhythm against her lips. "She asked how you were. If you were well and . . . and happy."

"What did you tell her?"

"I told her you were eating." Suddenly her eyes flew up to his. "Did you have dinner tonight?"

"I took a cab to Chinatown and ate at Kan's."

"Was it good?"

"Delicious, but too much for one person." His mouth quirked into a smile before it settled into lines of unbearable sadness.

She longed to touch it, to smooth away the tragedy she saw riding on it. It was a mouth designed to smile. Or to kiss. She tore her eyes away and said breathlessly, "I guess that's all. Good night." She brushed past him in the darkness.

"Sloan?"

"Yes?" she turned quickly to see him standing far too close. His breath stirred her hair. She could smell the bouquet of the after-dinner liqueur he had drunk.

"What did you tell her about the other?"

"Other?"

"About whether I was happy or not."

She couldn't be drawn away from the magnetism of his eyes. Her vocal cords failed her, but she managed to make herself heard. "I told her that you were working hard and concentrating on your book."

"Is that what you think I'm concentrating on?"

He watched the blue-gray eyes go glossy with emotion and wide with confusion and cloudy with longing. God, when she looked up at him like that, how was he supposed to control his longing to hold her in his arms? After having spent hours, days, nights, tasting nothing but her lips and breasts on his tongue, feeling nothing but the satiny warmth of her skin on his fingertips, hearing nothing but the erotic purring sound she had made deep in her throat when he touched her intimately, how could she be forbidden to him? He wanted to taste all of her, touch what had been promised beneath her clothes, hear her cries of ecstasy when the crisis came.

He had had only a preview of what it would be like to love her, yet he knew that beneath her serenity beat the heart of a passionate, giving lover, generous with her affections. His body ached when, against his better judgment, he let his imagination run free. Blood galloped through his veins when he imagined her naked beneath him, receiving all the love he had to give.

He thought he would die if he had to go through life never having known all of her. He was obsessed with the thought of her sweet mystery enfolding him snugly and warmly. She would take this surging hunger, that often beaded his forehead with sweat, and appease it. His erratic heart would be quieted. But his soul would soar.

Until then, he was consumed with relentless passion. He couldn't write, couldn't sleep. Still, his fantasies of loving her were more satisfying than the act had been with other women. He wasn't about to give them up. He'd go mad if he did. Just as he'd go mad thinking of her with any other man. The thought of her graceful, slender limbs twined around any body other than his sent him near the brink of sanity. If she were this passionate with him, wasn't it practical to assume . . . He had to ask, had to know.

"That salesman, Jason?"

"Yes?"

"You said you lived with him."

"Yes," she answered hoarsely.

"You slept with him, of course."

"Yes."

"Was he the first?"

"The only."

"Did he . . . did he make you . . . happy?"

"No."

She mouthed the word. The sound didn't carry past her trembling lips. He uttered an anguished groan and his hand came up to cradle her cheek. She tilted her head and leaned into his palm. His touch seemed to infuse her with a debilitating drug that robbed her of the will to move. She could only stand there and absorb the heat emanating from him as one soaks up the healing rays of the sun. It was a strange drug, for conversely it awakened the erogenous parts of her body while anesthetizing the rest of her. She could feel her breasts filling with love, the tips tingling with burgeoning desire. A delicious, lethargic warmth seeped through her feminine domain with a steady pulsing that echoed that of her heart. Of his.

"The man was a fool," Carter said huskily.

He ran his thumb once along the moist fullness of her lower lip before he heaved a sigh of taxing self-discipline and turned away. Her heart returned to its plodding, dejected cadence. It beat in time to his footsteps on the stairs.

Chapter Five

"I think that's selfish of you, Carter," Alicia said with her mouth beautifully pouting. "What difference does it make?"

"No one reads my manuscript before I'm finished. Completely finished. Not my agent, not my editor, not my . . . fiancée. No one."

They were in the dining room eating the meal Sloan had spent most of the day preparing. The food was delicious, the ambiance of the turn-of-the-century dining room warm and cozy, especially with the incessant rain that ran in silver rivulets down the paned windows. For once Sloan was eating her meal in the room. She had even dressed for the occasion in the same black skirt and georgette blouse she'd worn the first night Carter had been there. Her hair was swept up into a loose knot on top of her head. Pearl earrings adorned her ears. She looked as though she fit the room. Alicia did not.

She looked much too modern and sophisticated.

Sloan had been lighting the fire in the parlor when the brass knocker had announced her friend's arrival. Alicia had thrown herself into Sloan's arms and hugged her with characteristic ebullience. Carter had been treated to the same unrestrained affection when he came down the stairs, having heard her cheerful exclamations.

He had taken the lively Alicia in his arms and embraced her warmly, kissing her on the cheek as she wrapped her arms around his neck. Sloan had turned blindly back into the parlor on the pretext of checking the fireplace.

Alicia's blond hair had come through the flight, the rain and wind, her wild embraces without being disturbed. Her eyes danced with customary merriment. Her lips smiled as she chattered about the impossibilities involved in leaving children with grandma even for two days. When she came down to dinner after Sloan had showed her to her room—the one conveniently next to Carter's—she was wearing an electric blue silk hostess pajama set, having changed from her red wool pants and matching leather jacket.

Now her beautiful face was puckered with vexation. "Artistic temperament, I suppose. Do you understand why he won't at least let me thumb through his manuscript, Sloan?"

Sloan desperately wished Alicia wouldn't ask her opinion on anything concerning Carter. She toyed with the food remaining on her plate with an idle fork. "Yes, I think I can. He wants to make it as perfect as he knows how, and if he doesn't feel it's perfect yet, he's cheating both you and himself if he lets you read it prematurely."

Alicia looked at her as though she were speaking a foreign language. "I guess so. But for heaven's sake, I'm going to be his wife."

Carter, too, was looking at Sloan, and she hoped the light burning in his eyes was only a reflection of the candles on the table. "I'm sorry, Alicia. But

I remain steadfast. No one reads the book till I'm done."

"How much do you lack? Can you finish it earlier than you originally thought?"

He shifted uneasily in his chair and took a sip of wine. "I don't think so. I'm not happy with the last chapter."

"It's probably wonderful," Alicia said admiringly and reached across the table to cover his hand.

Envy stabbed through Sloan's vital organs. Alicia had the right to touch his hand. She had the right to brush back the unruly hair that had fallen onto his forehead, the right to trace the mismatched arches of his eyebrows, and to iron out with loving fingertips the worried crease between them. Did Alicia even see that flagrant sign of anxiety?

"There are certainly no noises or distractions here," Alicia said with a laugh. "What happened to the autumn tourist trade, Sloan?" she asked, turning away from her fiancé.

"I'm afraid the weather is keeping them all at home. The television reports have scared them. I had two separate reservations cancelled yesterday. A group of four women due to arrive next week called today to reschedule."

"Are you worried? I thought you were barely making it as it was."

Alicia wasn't being malicious, but Sloan could easily have throttled her for mentioning her rocky financial status. It was like pointing up another of her shortcomings. Alicia's family had always had money, as had Jim's. She had never known a lean day in her life. Sloan had never known a solvent one. "Oh, I'll survive," she said blithely. "I may have to start serving hot dogs rather than gourmet dinners, but I'll manage."

"Of course you will," Alicia said. "I wish I had one ounce of your competence and common sense."

I wish you did, too, Sloan thought to herself.

And I wish I gave off the impression of feminine frailty.

"Anyway," Alicia went on, "I'm glad you didn't start cutting back tonight. That ham was delicious." She folded her napkin beside her plate and stretched luxuriously. "Now I'm ready to curl up in front of the fire."

Sloan stood. "You and Carter make yourselves at home. I'll get started on the dishes."

"No, no, let me help," Alicia said.

"Go," Sloan said, pointing an imperious finger toward the parlor. "This is your mini-vacation. I'll have this done in no time and then I'll join you."

"You talked me into it," Alicia said, taking Carter's hand and leading him out of the room.

Sloan could feel his eyes on her as he went out, but she didn't look up from the tray she was piling with dirty dishes. She took a long time to clear things away, making breakfast preparations in the process. Done at last, she took off her apron and went reluctantly toward the parlor where she could hear Carter's rumbling laughter and Alicia's animated voice.

They were on the loveseat. Carter was sprawled in the corner while Alicia half-sat, half-reclined against him, her shoes off and her feet tucked under her thighs. She was fiddling with the buttons on his shirt. He'd taken his coat off.

"There you are. We'd about given up on you," Alicia said. "I was telling Carter about Adam's encounter with a mouse at his nursery school."

"Not too traumatic, I hope." Sloan took a chair across the room, trying to keep her eyes away from Carter's inscrutable face.

"More to the poor teacher than to Adam," Alicia said, laughing. She sighed and lay her cheek against Carter's chest, slipping her hand up to his throat. "Oh, this is so nice. Relaxing and peaceful. I can't tell you how those boys wear me out." She tilted her head up to look at Carter. "I needed to get away and see you so much."

He smiled down at her, kissed the end of her perfect nose, and lightly scratched the top of her head affectionately.

Sloan sprang out of her chair. "You two really must excuse me, but I'm extremely tired tonight. I think the rain is making me sleepy."

"But, Sloan—"

"We'll visit tomorrow, Alicia. I'm sure you'd rather be alone with Carter tonight. Please bank the fire and turn off the lights when you go upstairs. I'll see you both in the morning."

She fled the room, knowing it was rude, knowing she was a coward, and knowing that if she had stayed and watched them snuggled together on her loveseat, she would have died.

She hated herself for doing it. She stared at the door to Alicia's room and knew that if she opened it and found that Alicia's bed hadn't been slept in, she'd never forgive herself for being compelled to find out. But nothing on earth could keep her from seeing for herself where Alicia had spent the night. The brass knob turned under her hand and the door swung open and she saw the bed with its flung back spread and wrinkled sheets and dented pillow. One pillow.

Sloan weakly slumped against the doorjamb and immediately despised herself for this snooping. But she had *had* to know. She could excuse it as part of her job to go into a guest's bedroom to make the bed. Deep down, she knew she was spying on her best friend.

Last night she'd heard them as they went upstairs, but she hadn't been able to tell if they'd gone into the same room or not. It had been a hellish night. She'd tossed and turned in her bed imagining Alicia's beautiful naked body being explored by Carter's hands and lips. She could see his hard passion driving into Alicia's willing flesh, could feel each thrilling thrust as though it were she taking that glorious pounding. It had been all she could do to keep from screaming out her emotional agony.

They had come down to breakfast together, Alicia happy and vivacious and gorgeous, Carter rumpled and haggard and surly, as though he hadn't slept much.

"But at least he slept in his own room," Sloan said to herself as she quickly made Alicia's bed. The rest of the room was straight. Alicia was scrupulously tidy.

After the hearty breakfast Sloan had fed them, Alicia had insisted that Carter take her shopping. Despite her pleas, Sloan had declined to go with them, saying she had bookkeeping to do. She did, but it was nothing that couldn't be postponed or done in half an hour. Still, she couldn't punish herself by tagging along with them like a maiden aunt.

Sloan now went into Carter's room, which looked like it had suffered the ravages of a tornado. Balls of paper that hadn't made it into the trashcan were lying on the floor nearby. The table she'd provided him was littered with sheets of manuscript. Slashes of red ink crisscrossed them like bloody scratches. He was taking his clothes to a laundry within walking distance, but shirts and jeans and jackets and sweaters were draped over the furniture in postures resembling wounded bodies.

She began the chore of restoring order by making up the bed. Never had she been so grateful for having to do that task. She was folding one of his sweaters over a hanger when he walked into the room. She spun around, not having heard him come in the front door or up the stairs. But then she'd been absorbed with handling his clothes that smelled wonderfully of him and the cologne he always wore.

"What are you doing here?" she asked on a gasping whisper. Mindlessly she was clutching the sweater to her chest. She felt trapped, caught redhanded performing some shameful act.

"I live here," he said, the corner of his lip tilting into an amused smile.

"I mean where's Alicia?"

He shrugged out of his jacket and for once neatly hung it on the back of a chair. "At Saks in the couture department trying on clothes. I'd had enough and told her I'd meet her back here when she was finished. God knows when that could be."

Sloan remembered shopping expeditions she and Alicia had taken and knew her friend could occupy herself that way for hours. "She's having a good time," she said, turning to hang the sweater in the closet.

"I'm sorry about this room. I don't think I'm doing any permanent damage."

She smiled as she closed the closet door. "None at all. I make the beds and straighten the rooms each morning. Since you've got the largest room and are paying the most, it doesn't hurt me to hang up a few clothes."

"Thanks just the same."

"You're welcome."

The world dropped away as they stared at each other. They had been granted this small piece of the universe, this fraction of time in which to be alone. But such indulgences were hazardous to Sloan's aching heart and she felt it might shatter if she stayed with him a moment longer.

"I think that's everything for now," she said, edging toward the door. "I'll leave you alone so you can work." She reached the door without his stopping her, but when she would have pulled it open, his hand was splayed wide over it, keeping it shut.

"You look good in jeans."

She couldn't look at him. She stared at the back of his hand plastered to the door, preventing her from opening it. His knuckles were sprinkled with brown hairs and dotted with light freckles. She wanted to kiss them. Instead, she pretended she still had dominance over her faculties and could carry on ordinary conversation. "I don't wear slacks except sometimes on Saturday mornings when I do heavy cleaning."

"You don't smell like you've been cleaning. You smell like freshly baked bread." He moved closer, pressing his middle against her bottom.

She barely had sufficient breath to say, "I've been baking bread, too."

"I want a bite." He lowered his head and nudged her hair back with his nose. Then she felt his lips on the side of her neck, nibbling softly. His teeth raked her skin lightly. The spot was soothingly laved with his tongue as his mouth opened over it.

"Carter . . ." she breathed, ashamed and thrilled by the molten lava of desire that spilled from the center of her femininity to flow with delicious sluggishness through her veins.

"Do you have any idea how delectable your cute little butt looks in those jeans?" he asked in her ear as his tongue outlined its translucent rim. "No you don't, or you wouldn't wear them."

"You shouldn't say—"

"To hell with what I shouldn't say or with what I shouldn't do. I'm doing what I want to do for a change. And whether you admit it or not, it's what you want me to do. Isn't it? Say it, Sloan."

"Yes," she sobbed.

"Ah, God will damn us for sinners, but kiss me."

It was far more tender a kiss than she had

expected. He cupped her chin in his hand and turned her face around to his. Their mouths met over her shoulder. His lips parted and he drank of her for a moment before his tongue dipped into the silky depths of her mouth. When he withdrew it slowly, she murmured a protest. "Shhh, there's no hurry." He spoke against her lips, outlining them with the tip of his tongue.

With an indolent thumb, he stroked the underside of her chin and jaw. He used his tongue again, not urgently, but with a lazy and pumping motion that deflowered her mouth and made it entirely exclusively his.

"Raise your arms and put them behind my neck," he instructed as his lips left a string of scorching kisses along her throat.

She did as he asked of her, lacing her fingers through the hair that brushed his collar. It was natural to angle her body along his, to stretch against him, to rest her head on his chest.

His hands began a slow, circular massage up her ribcage. Responding to a pagan rhythm that thrummed through her body, she swayed slightly, rubbing her hips against the fly of his trousers. "My God, Sloan. Yes, love. Don't stop," he groaned.

With his head bending over her shoulder, he nuzzled his way along her shoulder, freeing the buttons of her blouse one at a time. Without haste, he peeled it away, taking the satin strap of her brassiere with it. He took love bites and sampled the texture and flavor of her skin with his tongue. He rubbed her with his chin, and the suggestion of his beard sent chills of delight racing through her body. Her fingers tightened in his hair and her back arched, lifting her breasts.

"So soft," he said, letting his hand find the top of her breast swelling over the cup of her bra. He filled his hand with her and rasped over the beguiling nipple with his fingertip. His eyes gleamed with masculine pride when it beaded beneath his coaxing. In no rush, he let his finger trace the circle of the pink areola. "This almost drove me nuts that first night. I wanted to do this." He gently rolled the bud of flesh between his fingers until its longing became more pronounced. "Then I wanted to touch it with my tongue." His voice dropped a decible, to little more than an aroused growl. "I still want to."

Sloan shivered with a seizure of uncontrollable passion when one lean, strong hand flattened over her abdomen and pressed her backward, urging her against his virility. Her muscles became gelatinous and she was plagued by a lassitude that she reveled in. She was sensuality's prisoner and Carter was the jailer. He held the key to all that made her woman. He had tapped the resource of her femininity and, like a well, it gushed forth, flooding her body, inundating her with sensations she had never experienced before.

"I want you, Sloan."

"I want you," she confessed on a ragged sigh, turning into his arms. Her arms snaked around his waist to hug him tight. She nestled her face on his chest, breathing deeply of his scent, knowing that within a few seconds she would have to let him go. But for a moment he was wanting her and she could pretend she belonged to him.

His lips moved in the mass of her hair as he held her to him, caressing through her jeans the taut, saucy derriere he'd admired. "After having made me suffer this purgatory, you'll love me now, won't you, Sloan?"

"I *do* love you," she vowed, letting her lips brush against his skin just beneath his collar.

He took her by the shoulders and pushed her away. His eyes impaled her. "You know what I mean."

"I'm not going to . . . to make love with you, no," she said quietly, but irrefutably.

He released her suddenly and slammed his fist

into the opposite palm. "Dammit," he cursed loudly. "Why?" Plowing deep furrows through his hair with angry fingers, he demanded again, "Why?"

Slowly, she readjusted her clothes and faced him with abject weariness. "You know why, Carter. Please let's don't go through this again. If we ever did . . . go to bed together, it would hurt someone we both dearly love."

"Are we hurting her any less by *wanting* to?"

"No, but we won't have to feel so guilty about it afterward."

"I doubt I'd ever feel guilty about giving you my love. And I sure as hell wouldn't feel guilty about taking yours."

"You would! I know you would."

Arrogantly, he hitched his thumbs under his belt. "Don't bet on it. I don't have the same perverse penchant for self-punishment that you have, Sloan. I don't get my kicks by being a martyr."

Anger surged through her veins where passion had flowed only moments before. "It seems I gave you more credit than you deserve."

"What's that supposed to mean?"

"I didn't think you'd resort to that masculine crutch. But if it placates your male ego to verbally abuse me because I turned you down, go ahead. It won't change my mind. I still won't go to bed with you."

"Abuse?" he scoffed. "Baby, let me tell you all about abuse. Abuse is when a woman strokes a man to rigid senselessness and then tells him it's no dice."

His words struck her in the stomach like vicious fists and made her nauseous. She swallowed scalding bile. "I don't like being called 'Baby,'" she ground through teeth clenched as tightly as her hands were. "And what you said is crude and vulgar."

His stance was one of goading belligerence. "I

haven't even gotten to the crudities and vulgarities yet."

"Save them for your book." She jerked open the door before firing her last insulting shot. "I'm sure they'll fit right in."

She slammed the door before he could make a comeback.

Alicia came in a short while later, lugging an armload of packages and boxes labeled distinctively from the exclusive stores of Union Square. "Sloan, Sloan," she called, bustling in after paying her cab fare.

Sloan came out of her office where she had been poring over the discouraging tapes her adding machine spat out. "Did you leave anything in the stores?" she asked, trying not to sound like she'd been kissing this woman's fiancé less than an hour ago. Alicia's bright, childlike face did nothing to alleviate her disgust with herself. Alicia's hair was rain-dampened and windblown and she was decked out in black patent boots and a matching vinyl raincoat.

"Wait until you see the absolutely gorgeous things I bought. Where's Carter?"

"Upstairs working," Sloan said, avoiding Alicia's eyes. "I can hear his typewriter."

"Come up. I want to try my things on for you."

"In a minute. Go on up. I'll bring some hot cider and you can give me a fashion show." She had to have more recuperative time. However, she didn't think all the time in the world would rid her of the guilt she felt.

"Okay," Alicia said as she happily tripped upstairs.

Carter's typewriter was silent when Sloan carried the tray up a few minutes later, but his door was closed. Alicia's was partially opened so Sloan pushed it with her foot as she went inside. She halted just inside the threshold, gripping the handles of the tray with knuckles gone white.

The packages and boxes were lying helter-skelter on the bed and floor. Carter and Alicia were standing in the middle of the room locked in an embrace that caused Sloan's heart to wrench painfully in her chest. Alicia's coat hung by one arm and shoulder as though she'd been arrested in the process of taking it off. Carter's hands were imbedded in her thick skein of blond hair. His mouth was working savagely over Alicia's.

Sloan felt she had been nailed to the floor. She was unable to move as her spirit deflated like a discarded balloon. Her eyes were wide and vacant with disillusionment as she stared at Carter's mouth devouring Alicia's with unleashed passion. Her own lips parted and a serrated sigh like a death rattle shuddered through them.

That's how Carter saw her when he jerked his head up from the dissatisfactory, bruising kiss. He dropped his arms from around Alicia as a spasm of self-loathing shook him. He had never felt so wretched in his life. Not only for the horrible expression he had brought to Sloan's face, but for the shabby way he had treated Alicia. She hadn't deserved that debasement. It wasn't her fault he was drowning in his own poison. The kiss had been to serve one purpose and one purpose only. And it hadn't stemmed from desire.

Alicia pressed shaky fingers to her mouth and turned, flustered, to see Sloan. "Oh, Sloan. We . . . Carter . . . he wants to see the things I bought, too. And . . . here, set that heavy tray down. You didn't have to serve refreshments, but then you're such a dear."

She chatted on, while Carter and Sloan moved mechanically and answered responsively as though the whole scene had been rehearsed and they all knew what roles they were supposed to play and what lines of dialogue to recite.

Sloan was never so relieved as when they said they wanted to go out for dinner. Of course they expected her to go with them, but she refused. Alicia pleaded. Carter was stonily silent after politely seconding Alicia's invitation. Sloan remained resolute, and finally Alicia gave up.

Alicia wore one of her new dresses and Carter looked handsome and successful in his sport coat and tie. The perfect couple. The embodiment of the American dream.

Sloan, smiling and commissioning them to have a good time, watched as they climbed into the cab. She closed the door to Fairchild House and pressed her head into the hard coldness of the door, wishing she had no more feeling than it.

Everything Carter had said had been a lie. He'd wanted a convenient bed partner, one last fling before he got married. That she was his fiancée's best friend, that the fiancée was underfoot, only made for intrigue. It was something fresh out of the pages of one of his novels. When Sloan had spurned his base advances, he'd run straight and sure back to Alicia's loving arms.

God, what a fool she'd made of herself. Twice. First she'd believed Jason could love her. Then she'd believed Carter did. If it weren't so tragic, her culpability would be laughable. Jason's rejection she'd taken with a stiff upper lip and a grim resignation that things were running true to form.

"Why does it hurt so much more this time?" she asked the walls of her room.

It wasn't easy to fall asleep, but she was almost afraid to anyway. She was afraid that if she closed her eyes, she might die of despair in the empty house.

"I think I'll go back to Los Angeles with you," Carter said quietly.

Sloan hadn't heard them last night when they

had come in. She was glad. She didn't want to know if they'd shared the same room during the night. Most probably they had. Carter's lust had been thwarted once by her untimely appearance. She doubted he'd have been deterred again.

Alicia had insisted on helping with the brunch dishes and now they were lazing away the hours of early afternoon with cups of coffee in front of the fire in the parlor.

Swearing all the while that she despised the real man Carter camouflaged behind his charm, his announcement nonetheless rattled Sloan's composure.

"Do you mean it, Carter?" Alicia asked excitedly. Sloan saw her hand grip his thigh with familiarity. "Oh, that's wonderful! David and Adam will—"

She broke off abruptly and collapsed against the back of the loveseat. "No," she grumbled. "You can't come back. Not now."

Sloan glanced at Carter but when she saw that his own surprise mirrored hers, she quickly averted her eyes back to Alicia's sullen face.

"Why shouldn't I go back home? I thought you'd want me to."

"I do, Carter," Alicia said earnestly. "But you haven't finished your book and you couldn't get it done before the wedding even if you locked yourself in your house. We'd all start hounding you just as we did before."

He shrugged. "I just won't finish it until after the wedding. It's not crucial that I meet my deadline. I can get an extension."

"Oh no," Alicia said, sitting up straighter and shaking her blond mane emphatically. "I'm not starting off a marriage with something as important as a literary masterpiece between us. You'd never forgive me for that."

"It's hardly a literary masterpiece. There would be nothing to forgive."

She looked at him with open skepticism. "I know

you, Carter Madison. If your book isn't going well,
you're miserable and I don't want a sad sack for a
groom. You tell him, Sloan. He should stay here
in Fairchild House until he's finished. Right?"

Sloan's eyes bounced from Alicia to Carter. He
was carefully listening for her answer. It was much
safer to look at Alicia. "I'm sure Carter will do
what he feels he should without any advice from
me."

"You like it here, don't you, Carter? Sloan's not
mistreating you, is she?" Alicia asked teasingly.

Sloan's face paled, but Carter answered swiftly.
"No, no, it's nothing like that. It's just that no
book is as important as you and the boys."

"You really should go ahead and finish it, darling.
You won't be happy until you do, will you?"

His eyes made a swift trip in Sloan's direction
and back. "No," he admitted at last.

"And this is the best place for you to work right
now. So you'll stay, though I truly appreciate your
making the unselfish gesture." Alicia leaned over
and planted a soft kiss on his mouth. He touched
her shoulder briefly. "Now I've got to get my things
together. The cab will be here in less than an
hour."

Sloan watched the cab pull away, Alicia waving
enthusiastically from the back seat. The car was
soon swallowed by the gloom and the rain. Carter
preceded Sloan into the house and went into the
parlor. He was standing in front of the fireplace
gazing into the flames when he said, "I tried."

She had been making a hasty retreat toward
her own quarters when his words stopped her.
The tension between them was palpable. How they
were going to survive until the next guests arrived
at Fairchild House, she didn't know.

"What did you say?"

He turned around, a dark, slender silhouette

against the firelight. He hadn't turned on any lamps. The room and hall were dark save for the reddish glow. "I said I tried. To gracefully leave," he added when she still seemed not to comprehend.

"Yes, well . . . It would have been best. I think this is the first time in her life Alicia made a decision with her head instead of her heart." She said it with derisive affection and he caught the humor. It served to lessen the tension somewhat.

He chuckled softly. "Her timing is off." He studied the carpet beneath his feet. "She's a trusting soul. She doesn't suspect a thing. She didn't even mention that we'd be here alone without any customers for chaperones."

Sloan looked away and crossed her arms in front of her. She was suddenly very cold. "She has no reason to mistrust either of us."

He sighed heavily. "No. I guess not." She grew warm again when he stopped pretending interest in the rug and raised his eyes to her. They shone on her from across the dim room. "Can you trust me, Sloan?"

"What do you mean?" The convulsive working of her throat made her voice sound unnatural.

"Yesterday. I wanted to take you to bed and you said no and I got mean and insulting. God!" He thumped his fists against his thighs. "I don't know what made me act like that. I've never been that abusive with a woman before. If she said no, I'd tip my hat and be on my way, but with you . . ." He looked at her hopelessly and lifted his arms in appeal. "I just can't seem to take no for an answer. I was angry, physically agitated, not a little frustrated and . . . I'm sorry. Please forgive me."

She twisted her hands at her waist. "I'm as much to blame as you, Carter. You were justified to be angry. I led you to believe that I was more than willing."

"Sloan, you know I'd never hurt you, don't you?"

Her head shot up at his agonized tone. "Of course," she pledged with soft urgency.

"You know I'd never force—"

"Yes!"

He went to a chair and dropped down, linking his hands loosely between wide-spread knees. "You saw me kissing Alicia." It wasn't a question, but a simply stated fact.

Again she felt that pain, like a spear piercing her heart. "That's what men are supposed to do with their fiancées. Kiss them."

"But they're not supposed to be in the hope of banishing another woman from their mind." He looked up at her from where he sat, his hair falling with disregard over his creased forehead. "They don't kiss them wishing they could forget how delicious another woman tastes."

"Oh, Carter, please stop." Sloan covered her face with both hands.

"That's the only reason I was kissing poor, startled Alicia. I promise you she's never known such unbridled lust. At least not from me. I had to see if I could find a trace, only a trace, of the pleasure kissing you gives me. It was a stupid thing to do. Naturally there was none. Because she isn't you."

"Don't tell me this," she cried.

"I don't know how I'll ever make love to her after we're married." He came out of the chair, across the room to her, and pulled her hands free from her tear-bathed face. "Maybe I'll pretend she is you."

"No!" She whirled around, giving him her back. The tears that had longed to be released for days ran down her cheeks. He turned her to face him again, but not as a lover, as a friend.

"Weep for both of us, Sloan," he whispered. He pressed her wet face into his shirt front and comforted her as he would a child while she continued to cry. He stroked her hair and rubbed her neck and smoothed his hands down her back.

She let him. Because she never remembered a time when someone had comforted her. She'd always been there for other people to pour out their sorrow to, but had never been allowed the luxury of revealing her disappointments. Under Carter's loving hands and melodic reassurances, she gave vent to all her brokenheartedness.

"We won't speak of it anymore, Sloan. You've been right all along. I know my obligation, what I have to do, and it's unfair of me to hurt you like this. So we won't ever be lovers, but I'd like very much to be your friend. And as a friend, I ask you a favor."

She lifted drenched eyes to his. He swiped lingering tears from her cheeks with the caressing pads of his thumbs. "What favor?"

"Would you read my manuscript?"

Chapter Six

She knew her expression must define imbecilic. She could feel her mouth hanging slack and her eyes blinking rapidly. Carter saw the amazement on her face and seemed pleased by it because he grinned in that lopsided, endearing way of his.

"But you said no one ever reads a manuscript of yours before it's finished," she gulped out between lips that were operating like a goldfish's.

"No one does. This is an exception. I want you to read *Sleeping Mistress* and tell me what you think of it . . . honestly."

"I didn't know you were finished with it."

"I'm not. That's why I want you to read it. I'm having trouble with the last chapter. Maybe if you read the rest of the book and give me your observations, something in my head will click."

After a moment of introspection she said slowly, "Alicia will be upset."

"She'll never know. At least I don't intend to tell her you've read it."

Her eyes roamed aimlessly over his face while she pondered her decision. They lingered on the wayward hair that graced the top of his ears. That, like everything about him, made her want to touch him. "Alicia should be the one who reads the manuscript for you." Sloan never wanted to be accused of usurping Alicia's place in his life.

"She would love it, or rather she'd tell me she loved it whether she did or not. And that's not to be taken as a criticism of her. It's a truthful observation. She'd be kind at the risk of offending me."

"How do you know I wouldn't do that? Tell you what you want to hear instead of what I really think."

He laughed then, a deep, rich sound that surrounded her with warmth, that she would bask in. "You've never minced words with me before, nor shied away from saying things I didn't particularly want to hear. Even at the risk of making me furious. I don't imagine you'd start now." He saw the pros and cons parading across her face in stark disclosure of her indecision. "It won't take up too much of your time, will it? You could do it in the evenings."

She laughed then. "I don't suppose I'll be busy this week. You're my only boarder."

"Speaking of that, don't go through that servile hostess routine just for me, okay? You're lovely when you do it. I've never see anyone handle things so competently and graciously. But let me treat you to some meals out." When he saw she was about to object he stopped her with raised palms. "I insist. It can be your payment for reading the manuscript."

"But your breakfast and dinner are included in the price of the room."

"Then we'll consider it a swap off."

"Your meals are worth more than that," she argued.

"God, you're proud and stubborn. Okay, let's say you can fix my breakfast and serve it in the *kitchen*, and we'll either go out or have sandwiches or something easily prepared for dinner. Deal?"

He stuck his hand out for her to shake. She took it and pumped it twice firmly. "Deal."

"Sealed with a handshake and"—he leaned down toward her—"a kiss."

His lips met hers softly, but firmly, in what was supposed to be a dispassionate kiss. Instead the contact of his mouth on hers sent an arrow of love shooting into her body. It imbedded itself deep in her womb and splintered through her whole being. Their lips never opened, their tongues remained dormant, the kiss never expanded into one of unleashed desire. Yet they valued it more than any other they had shared. It was a declaration not of the physical desire they had for each other, but of the spiritual need that was also having to be denied. That sacrifice was the hardest to bear.

When he pulled away, his sherry-colored eyes were misty with longing. "When do you want to start?" he asked thickly.

"Tonight."

He smiled, realizing that all her objections had been for show. His heart swelled with pride over how eager she was to read his manuscript.

Sloan's own heart was exultant. He was granting her a privilege no one else had ever had, nor ever would. It wasn't his body, or his name, or even his love. It was his life's work he was giving her. And she knew that above all else, that was most precious to him.

"Well, are you going to make me beg?" he asked from the kitchen table the next morning. She was at the range scrambling eggs.

"I'm punishing you for coming to the kitchen to eat. Breakfast is part of our deal, remember? I planned to bring it up to you on a tray."

He sipped his coffee. "I've been up for hours, pacing that room until I thought it was a decent enough hour to come downstairs. How far did you you read?"

"Eat your eggs," she said, thumping the plate down in front of him and swinging away saucily.

He muttered an imaginative curse, but attacked the plate of food while she ate at a more sedate pace. Sitting across the breakfast table from him, each dressed casually, alone in the house, she indulged herself and fantasized that it wasn't temporary, that Alicia didn't exist. Fairchild House was empty save for them, yet to Sloan it had never felt cozier. It seemed to have shrunk in the rain, to have formed a chrysalis around them that sealed them off from the rest of the world.

"What did you think of the first chapter?" he asked around a mouthful. "Did you read the first chapter at least?"

"The weather man said we're in for at least three more days of rain." Being deliberately obtuse, she meticulously spread jam on her biscuit.

"All right, all right, I get the point," he grumbled. "Pass the bacon, please."

When they were done, she carried their plates to the sink, ran hot water over them, and came back to the table bringing the coffee pot with her. She refilled their cups. Carter watched each move impatiently, tapping his thumbnail against the stem of his eyeglasses.

"Your first chapter is excellent," she said after taking a contemplative sip of coffee.

His shoulders sagged in relief, but he tensed back up immediately. "You're not just saying that?" The glasses were shoved to the top of his head where they rode most of the time he wasn't actually working.

Her laugh was full throated and wholesome. "No." She shook her head. "I thought the man running down the alley in terror of the man who was chasing him was going to be the hero."

"That's what you were supposed to think."

"The way you described his ringing footsteps on the dark wet streets, the thudding heartbeat . . . well, you know what you wrote. Anyway, I thought you set the scene perfectly. I was feeling his fear, his panic. My lungs were bursting just as his were. I was thoroughly surprised—"

"When he turned out to be the bad guy and the man chasing him was the hero."

"Yes! That was an extremely clever twist. The readers will love it. But—"

"But what?" he asked anxiously.

She shuddered. "Did you have to make his murder so brutal and bloody?"

He grinned. "It wasn't a murder, it was an execution. He was a Nazi guilty of atrocities. Besides, the hero has to be not only heroic, but dangerous. A shade beyond the pale. A large percentage of my reading audience is men. The books are a fantasy for them. And when someone's brains are blown out against a brick wall by a .357 Magnum, it's a lot more grisly than I described it. There's really no way to describe it."

She swallowed hard. "Y—you've seen . . . that?"

"Yeah. A buddy of mine is with the FBI and when I told him what I needed, he called me the next time—"

"I don't think I want to know anymore," she said quickly.

"Okay," he said smiling. "Is that as far as you got? The first chapter?"

"Through chapter four. And I like it, Carter."

"Do you? Really?"

"Really. Cross my heart." She made the childish gesture, but the gleam in his eyes as they followed the path her finger took between the lush mounds of her breasts was most adult.

As though they had adhered there, he had to peel his eyes away from her breasts to lift them back to her face. "I know it's a mess. Can you read it okay? I've been making revisions right and left since I got here. When I haven't been able to work on that last chapter, I've been attacking the rest of it with a vengeance."

"I had trouble following the editing marks in some spots, but I deciphered them well enough. The story moves so quickly and you've put the hero in an impossible situation. I can't wait to see how you're going to get him out of it." The animation that had made her face beautifully mobile, suddenly fell away as though a mask had been removed. "He's not going to die or anything, is he?"

He chuckled at her obvious distress. "No, he's not going to die."

"In that case, I can't wait to get back to it. Are you going to work today?"

"Yeah. I'm going to change a scene in chapter six before you get to it."

She had cleared the table as they talked and was now stooping to load the dishwasher. She had no idea how provocative her pose was from the back. "Why?"

"You've given me an inspiration."

She turned around, her fingers dripping water onto the spotless floor. "*I* have?"

"I told you I liked you in jeans. I want to put them in the book."

Self-consciously, she dried her hands on a dishtowel, not quite able to meet Carter's eyes. "I only wore jeans today because no one else is here and I need to do some regrouting in one of the showers."

"Don't apologize for looking sexy as hell in a pair of jeans, Sloan," he said softly.

With an attack of shyness, she tucked a strand of hair behind her ear. "I didn't . . . I mean *I* don't think I look . . . sexy as . . . as hell."

His eyes lasered into her from across the room and held her motionless. "I know. You don't work at it. That's what makes it so effective."

She might be able to stand what he was saying if he weren't saying it in that voice that reminded her of a mink glove. She'd seen it advertised in the back pages of a magazine. It was a toy, a sexual toy, designed for lovers to wear while giving each other a massage. That's what Carter's voice felt like as it stroked her ears. Mink on naked skin.

She tried not to think of it on her bare stomach and between her thighs as she stammered, "H–how can you use my . . . uh . . . jeans in your book?"

"I have Gregory getting shot in the shoulder at the end of chapter five. He wanders around in this labyrinth of a Swiss village, dazed with fever, and in pain. Lisa, who sees him in chapter four making a contact, has been following him."

"I've read that part."

He nodded. "When he finally faints from loss of blood, she has him carried up to her apartment and tends to his wound herself. He's delirious for days." He shrugged self-critically. "Trite, but effective. Anyway, when he starts to regain consciousness, I had her bending over him looking like an angel. He sat up and lay his head against her breasts like he was trying to decide if he was still alive or not. He got . . . uh . . . well, he responded to her physically, and knew he wasn't dead."

"I don't see anything wrong with that." Sloan stared at him entranced. She couldn't look away from his magnetic eyes any more than she could keep from walking toward him where he still sat in the chair at the table.

"It was okay." Carter cleared his throat of an

unusual raspiness. "But instead, I think I'll have him open his eyes and the first thing he sees is this terrific feminine derrière in a pair of tight jeans. Lisa can be bending over the end of the bed, tucking in the covers around his feet or something. Yeah, that's it," he said with a spurt of inspiration, "because he's had fever and when it began to break, he kicked the covers off.

"He reaches up and touches her . . . fanny . . . like he can't really believe it's there, like it must be a part of his dream." Carter matched action to words and molded his hand to Sloan's hip. "He caresses it. It's firm and round and taut. She knows what's going on in his mind and stands perfectly still, letting him do what he will to reassure himself that he's still alive."

Carter was kneading her gently, rhythmically, and Sloan swayed unsteadily, intoxicated by his words and touch. Instinct alone brought her hands to his hair to remove the eyeglasses. Solicitously she smoothed back the mahogany strands and stroked his brow with comforting fingertips, as though he had been the one raging with fever.

"Then he brings his hand around to her front and presses it . . . here." He looked at her abdomen. The long tail of her unglamorous shirt was knotted at her waist. He lay his hand along the fly of her jeans. The tip of his middle finger was on the metal snap and the heel of his hand adjusted itself over the soft swelling femininity.

"Eventually," he went on in that mesmerizing voice that held her spellbound in a web of sensuality, "he unsnaps her jeans and lowers the zipper."

He didn't move, but actuality couldn't have been more potent than the power of his words. Sloan closed her eyes. She could see it. Feel it happening.

"He lowers the zipper slowly until he comes to the lacy band of her bikini panties. He smiles, a half-amused, half-fearful smile, because this may still be an hallucination. Then he touches her skin with his fingertips, brushing them back and forth across her abdomen. Her skin is vibrating with life and it shimmies up through his fingers, telegraphing him that he's alive too. With a small groan he raises himself to a sitting position and lays his head against her, pressing his mouth to the woman flesh that is so soft and smooth and smells so good. He kisses her navel, probes it with his tongue."

Involuntarily Sloan whimpered and, though his hand was motionless and her skin was still covered, her flesh quivered reflexively and she could feel the damp strokings of his tongue over her navel.

"He nuzzles her, catches her panties between his teeth, and scrapes his tongue along the lacy edge. He sighs in relief. She's not an illusion. His head flops back down on the pillow and his hand falls to the bed." Carter's hand dropped from her to dangle loosely at his side. She removed her hands from his temples where her fingers had been sifting through the burnished strands of dark hair.

Carter's sigh was one of sublime peace and his whisper was a lullaby. "He closes his eyes and sleeps, knowing that because she exists, because she's real, because she's there with him, he will survive."

Ponderous seconds ticked by until he roused himself out of his fantasy and looked up at her. "How does it feel to be a Muse?"

"I'm honored," she said in a thready voice. She shook herself slightly, trying to throw off the cloak of eroticism he had blanketed her with. Her legs threatened to give way and she stumbled away from the table. It became essential that she put distance between them. "But this Muse has a shower to regrout and a contrary curtain rod to tamper with."

It was a desperate effort on Sloan's part to put

things aright, to clear away the marvelous debris of an emotional storm. It was a brave, valorous gesture, but her lips were tremulous and her eyes were shimmering with tears. She would valiantly fight for the cause even if her heart wasn't in it.

He was merciful and followed her lead to let go the fantasy before it became reality. Grudgingly, but with the same spirit of bravado, he said, "And this writer has chapters to revise and one to compose."

They went to their separate jobs, but it was a long time before either of them was able to concentrate on anything but the scene they had enacted.

"This is insane, Carter."

"Come on. Just a few more yards. Where's your sense of adventure?"

"Back in my living room where it's warm and dry . . . and light. How can you see?"

"Night vision. Hey, that'd be a terrific title, wouldn't it? *Night Vision* by Carter Madison. I like that. Guess what, Granny. We're here."

She looked around her and saw only stygian darkness through a drizzling rain. "Where?"

"At the bench on the top of the hill."

Evening had already fallen when he had bounded down the stairs, telling her to grab a coat and hat and follow him. She'd obeyed and was amazed when he insisted on driving. Asking where they were going gained her nothing because he wouldn't tell her. He stopped at a convenience store and bought a loaf of sourdough bread, a bottle of red wine, a block of cheese, and a package of cold cuts. They drove across the Golden Gate Bridge. Immediately upon reaching the Sausalito side, he had taken a left turn, driven through a long, absolutely black tunnel, then up a winding road to the ridge of a hill looming over the bay.

"We walk from here," he had said as he pulled on the emergency brake of her car.

"Walk?" she had asked in a high, disbelieving voice. "To where?"

"To the top."

Now he was pulling her down beside him onto a cold, hard bench and making a broad sweep with his arm. "There, Ms. Fairchild, lies before you the finest view of San Francisco."

To their right and slightly behind them was the Pacific Ocean, dark and ominous and shrouded with fog. The mournful hoot of foghorns on the boats and tugs that had defied the dreadful weather sounded haunting in the dreary stillness. To their left and in front of them San Francisco had been set like a jewel mounted on the hilly terrain. In the immediate foreground Sloan could see the skeletal shadow of the Golden Gate bridge, its lights fuzzy and diffuse.

"There before me lies the finest view of San Francisco totally obliterated by rain and fog," she said dryly.

"You'll feel better after a cold slice of bologna," he said commiseratingly, a laugh lurking just behind his lips.

They munched on the hard bread, tearing at it with their teeth and then storing it beneath Sloan's poncho to keep it dry. The block of cheese was passed back and forth as was the bottle of wine.

"You got to read some this afternoon?" he queried with affected nonchalance.

"Yes. It felt downright sinful to be reading a book when I'm usually cleaning or cooking, but I was so enthralled I didn't even care."

"Good. It's healthy for a body to be sinfully self-indulgent every once in a while. Despite the less than ideal weather conditions, you needed this outing tonight, too. Having fun?"

She looked up at him and smiled languorously.

"Yes," she said softly. "I'm having a wonderful time."

He looked at her mouth. It was so beautiful when she smiled naturally and openly, not with the guarded austerity she imposed on herself. The darkness made it impossible for him to be sure, but he thought her lips had been stained rosy from the wine. He couldn't think of anything tastier, more inebriating, more sexually stimulating than licking the taste of wine from her lips. He dragged his mind away from that to save his sanity. "What about the book?"

"It's pure entertainment, Carter. But it has pathos, too."

"It didn't until I made those recent changes. Go on."

"I love it. I think it's the best you've ever done."

"Truthfully?"

"Truthfully."

"There's only one scene that bothered me." She snuggled down deeper in her poncho. The wind off the ocean was frigid against her back.

"Cold?"

"A little," she admitted.

"Here." He pushed her off the bench, scooted over, and then pulled her down onto his lap. "I'll be your windbreak. Stretch out."

He sat with his long legs stretched out in front of him in a half-reclining position, bracing his shoulders on the back board of the bench. She aligned her body to his and gradually let him absorb her weight. "How's that?" he asked in her ear.

His breath was hot against her rain-damp skin. "Better." It was blissful. Despite the rain and the cold and their meager supper, she'd never felt more relaxed and fulfilled and comfortably warm in her life.

"Have another sip of wine," he urged, passing her the bottle under her arm. She took a long draught, which she didn't think she needed because her head was buzzing and her body was heavy with a deliciously sapping lethargy. His arms slipped around her beneath the poncho and pulled her close against him. The hard impression of him was firm against the cleft of her buttocks. "Now what part bothered you?"

She didn't think her floating mind could form a coherent thought, drunk as she was by the arousing juxtaposition of their bodies. Carefully, her lips formed the words transmitted by her brain. "You know the scene where he comforts her after they escape from the terrorists?"

"At that old inn?"

Thoughtful fingers were strumming against her stomach. Her throat was aching from suppressing moans of animal pleasure. "Yes. Well, I think you might have short-changed it." The words tripped over each other on their breathless exit. "But who am I to tell you? I don't know anything about writing."

"I'm not offended. I asked. Go ahead."

His hand rested, palm upturned, just below her breast. "Lisa's emotions are riding right on the surface. She's been terrorized, she's experienced the exhilaration of escaping with her life, with Gregory's life."

His hands stirred and, if he had clamped them over her mouth, it couldn't have stifled her speech any more effectively.

"Go on." The murmur was actually no more than a wisp of air drifting across her ear.

"T—that scene where he comforts her after she realizes her child was actually killed in the raid . . ."

"Um-huh." His lips were moving against her lobe now. Not quite kisses, the meanderings were alluring enough to make her insides churn.

"You handled that beautifully. That's what she needed then. Comfort without romance. But in this other scene I don't think comfort would be enough."

"How do you mean?"

"You have him holding her. She's frantic, clinging to him almost hysterically. Then he just kisses her and she falls asleep. I'm not sure she wouldn't want something more, wouldn't want . . ."

"Intercourse?"

Her heart somersaulted and only then did she realize that it was gently imprisoned by his palm. Her nipple was nestled in the fleshy part of his hand while his fingers were curved around the full, soft globe with unqualified possessiveness. Even through the yarn of her sweater, she could feel his heat burning into her flesh, branding her heart with his name.

"Yes," she replied on the merest breath of sound. "I think she'd seek the ultimate outlet for the explosive emotions inside her. I think she'd want to celebrate that they were both alive in the most tumultuous way."

"You think I should have him make love to her?"

"Yes. Quickly, fiercely, almost brutally." She didn't know that her muscles were demonstratively contracting with each word, responding to the passion of the scene she envisioned, until she felt her hips squeezing against Carter's lap and heard his sharp intake of breath.

"God—" He hissed a vile curse and buried his face in the nape of her neck. "God, Sloan, you don't realize what you're doing." His breath was hot and rampant against her neck as he struggled for control. She, too, was finding it hard to regain mastery over emotions and senses plunged into chaos.

When at last the turbulence subsided, he kissed the side of her neck with utmost tenderness. "That's good advice, Sloan, very good." His fingers curled slightly and she felt her nipple hardening beneath the increased pressure. "It would work.

Gregory only pulled back out of concern for her. When they first realized they'd made good their escape, I described his desire for Lisa at great length."

She hiccupped a laugh and covered her mouth, ashamed at the *double entendre* that had sprung into her mind. Hopefully Carter wouldn't catch it.

He did. Placing his mouth against her ear, he said with a lascivious inflection, "Your mind is in the gutter, Ms. Fairchild. Did you find a pun in my choice of words?" She giggled again and he laughed. "You're tipsy. The prim and proper mistress of the respectable Fairchild House is actually drunk and not a little ribald in her private musings." He stood up, catching her under rubbery arms to bring her to her feet. "I'd better get you home before we catch pneumonia."

They were both relieved that the former tension had been banished, but his arm was firm around her waist as he led them down the steep, pebbly incline. At the car, he gave her a loud, smacking kiss. "Thanks for the help. I'll change the scene first thing tomorrow."

The day following their unorthodox picnic passed much as the preceding one had. They shared breakfast in the kitchen. Carter went back upstairs to his typewriter and Sloan decided to polish the silver. Off and on during the day, she read several pages of the manuscript, then a few more. She had become totally engrossed in the story and in the characters Carter had so admirably created.

He declared at mid-afternoon when he came down for a cup of coffee that he was taking her out to dinner.

"Indoors?" she cooed sarcastically.

He kissed her swiftly as he passed her on his way back upstairs. "Indoors. Someplace that has tables and chairs and everything."

The rest of the day she worked on herself, doing her nails, her hair, taking a long soaking bath in oil-slicked water, pressing her best dress. It was a soft, clinging wool jersey in a subdued shade of blue that deeped the mysterious hue of her eyes.

Carter couldn't help but notice that now, as he watched her from across the candlelit table. He had selected one of the restaurants at Pier 39 that overlooked part of the marina. Sailboats and cabin cruisers rocked dejectedly in the water, looking desolate and deserted in the rain-dimmed night.

"Carter, have you ever been married?"

"No, I've never been married. I came close once."

"What happened?" A sudden rush of color painted two bright patches on her cheeks. "You don't have to tell me," she added hastily. "I can't imagine why I asked."

He took her hand and squeezed it playfully. "You wanted to know. There's no heartbreaking secret as to why I'm still single. She was a bright, beautiful young lady, a decorator with a growing list of impressive clients. She wanted me to use my architecture degree and start making tubs of money so we could play hard and live fast. I wanted to write even if it meant not making any money and not playing so hard and living quite so fast. In short, we wanted different things, had irreconcilable goals, and we parted amiably."

"Where is she now?"

"Married to a bright and beautiful surgeon and living as she wanted to."

"But I'll bet her bright and beautiful surgeon doesn't make the money you do," she said in a sing-song voice.

He assumed a disbelieving look and his eyebrow shot up. "Why, Ms. Fairchild, I'm flabbergasted. Could it be that you have a malicious streak to your otherwise flawless nature?"

They laughed and declined the waiter's offer for more coffee. As they crossed the footbridge over

Embarcadero to the parking lot, she said. "I didn't know you had an interest in architecture."

"I studied it for five long, tedious years to please a father who thought wanting to be a writer was an unambitious copout."

"What does he think now?"

"Now he displays my books on the mantel like trophies. He and Mother live in Palm Springs. He's a retired banker."

"Do you love them?"

He paused and studied her for a long time before he said quietly. "Yes. Because they gave me life and because they did the best they knew how to do at parenting an only child. I see their short-comings and was frustrated and mad as hell when they laughed at my dreams. Now I take a little credit for myself for what I've become and try not to blame them for all that I'm not."

She cocked her head to one side. "Is there a lecture in there somewhere?"

The corner of his mouth tilted into a smile. "You're not only beautiful, you're perceptive." His expression changed as he framed her face between his hands and said seriously, "Just because your parents weren't capable of showering you with affection doesn't mean you're not worth loving, Sloan. It wasn't a failure on your part, but on theirs. They cheated themselves of your love. Don't cheat yourself."

Tears glistened on her eyelashes and there was a distinct tremor to the lips that whispered, "Thank you." Coming up on her toes, she kissed his hard cheek.

His eyes were like torches burning in the gloomy night as he said tightly, "You're welcome."

Tears blurred the last few lines of typed text, but she read each poignant word. She lowered the sheet of paper to her lap, then on impulse, flattened it against her breasts. It couldn't be wrinkled any more than it was. The corners were curled. There were markings and deletions and additions scribbled in the margins, but what was written on the page couldn't have been finer had it been engraved on silver.

They had returned home from their dinner out. Carter had bade her a regretful good night and gone upstairs. The remaining chapters of the manuscript lay so temptingly in their box that after Sloan had changed into her velour robe, she took it with her into the parlor. Stoking up the fire that had been banked before they left for dinner, and wrapping herself in a blanket for extra warmth, she got comfortable in one of the roomier chairs. Only one small lamp burned on the table at her elbow, but the whole room faded into oblivion as she stepped into the final scenes of Carter's book as though they were three dimensional.

His characters breathed. Sloan was wildly in love with Gregory, even as much as Lisa was. Indeed, the closer to the end of the book she got, the closer Lisa resembled her in how she thought and how she reacted to life.

By the time she got to the scene they'd played out in Carter's bedroom that first morning, she felt like she'd written the story. Not that she could have told it so expertly, but Carter had captured her ambiguity, her emotions, her physical cognizance of him, as keenly as if she'd quoted it to him verbatim. How could he know her so well? Secret thoughts she'd harbored were vividly revealed in Lisa's thought processes. Yet such blatant intrusion into her innermost self didn't feel like a violation. It felt like freedom.

Carter had actually seen the person she was behind the screen of caution she used for protection. Just as Gregory had coaxed Lisa's secrets from her, so had Carter brought all that Sloan Fairchild was out into the open.

He had read her soul, touched it, expressed it with words both lancing and sweet. She couldn't feel closer to him if they shared the same heart. They were one in the spirit. They couldn't be more an integral part of each other unless . . .

Her eyes sought him as though beckoned to do so. He was standing in the shadows near the doorway, barefoot and shirtless. He was still wearing the dress slacks he'd worn to dinner. His expression was indiscernible in the darkness.

Carter knew he'd never seen a more beautiful sight. She looked like a child folded in the chair with the blanket swathing her. Her feet were tucked under her. Her posture may have been innocent, but her rapt expression was that of a woman.

His heart jumped to his throat as he noted that her hands were pressing the last page he'd written to her breasts. He'd been unable to go any farther, but he'd worked on that damn passage for one whole day, trying to get it right, trying to capture Lisa's feelings on paper. Did Sloan recognize herself?

Were those tears in her eyes? They sparkled like liquid diamonds in the firelight. Her hair was alive with light. He'd noticed that she didn't peel it back anymore, but let it flow wild and free about her shoulders. He hadn't mentioned it or complimented her on it for fear she'd revert back to that blasted bun on the back of her head. Now firelight shone through the riotous curls. He longed to warm his hands in them.

He didn't move as she carefully lowered the sheet of paper back into the manuscript box. He remained in mute and motionless enchantment as she unwound her legs from the blanket and stood up.

His pulse rate accelerated to an alarming rate and his lips parted to facilitate his rushing breath when he saw her hand go to the zipper of her robe. He watched her slim fingers close around the tassel and tracked them as she lowered it—God!—past her navel. Only a slender ribbon of skin was revealed to him, but to gaze at it was an intimate act of love. He saw the graceful length of her throat, the valley between her breasts, their plump inner curves, the haunting groove that divided her stomach, her indented navel, and . . .

Dragging his eyes up from the shadowy mystery of her body, his eyes locked with hers. She smiled beseechingly as she peeled the robe from her shoulders and let it drop to her ankles.

He heard his own rattling whisper of praise for her naked perfection. She was Venus, infused with life, injected with fire. The dancing firelight licked her body with prurient delight. Everywhere the golden flickering light touched, he wanted to know with his hands, his mouth, his tongue. He felt himself filling, swelling with a love so strong it could only be granted fulfillment inside her body.

He was moving toward her even before he heard her whispered plea.

"Carter, love me."

Chapter Seven

"Gladly, my love, gladly," he said upon reaching her and clasping her to him. His hands sank into the mass of her hair and lifted her mouth for his fervent kiss.

His lips slanted over hers with tender possessiveness. "You can't imagine how lovely you are. I love the way you look, love your gorgeous body." His breath was warm, his words a love song against her lips. "Your mouth is so sweet. Give it to me to taste."

He nibbled at it with his own moist lips. His tongue probed at the corners, then glided without haste along her full bottom lip. When he prized her lips open, his tongue barely breached them and surveyed their slick lining with an analytical precision.

She whimpered her impatience and he raised his head slightly to tease her. "You hot little hussy."

"Yes, yes. For you I am. Kiss me." She wound her arms around his neck and curved her body up to interlock with his. Wantonly she moved against him in open invitation. His eyes went dark and a muscle in his cheek twitched.

One strong hands played wide over her hips and shoved her harder against him. The breath left her body in a long, corrugated sigh just as his lips opened over hers. His tongue pressed home, penetrating her mouth, filling it, stroking it with passion given vent.

She clawed at his hair with one greedy hand while the other examined the muscles that rippled beneath the tanned skin of his back.

Again and again his tongue assaulted her mouth, driving deeper each time. She denied him nothing. Their chests rose and fell together as they began to crave oxygen. He rested his mouth on hers as their breath was exchanged on rapid pants.

She didn't allow him to languish long, but coaxed him back, teasing his tongue with the tip of hers until his was once again inside her mouth. This time she became the aggressor. The sweet folds of her mouth tightly captured his tongue and she sucked it with a seductive rhythm.

Her breasts absorbed the vibrating growl inside his chest and she gloried in her ability to bring him such pleasure. He jerked his head back in surprise. "Good God, Sloan. I thought I was the master of symbolism."

"You're my master." Her fingertips smoothed over his damp lips, his cheekbones, his mismatched brows. The love radiating from the core of her soul made her eyes luminous. "Master me."

His eyes drilled into her the profound message of his own love. Taking up the blanket, he spread it out in front of the hearth on the carpet warmed by the fire. "Lie down on your back," he instructed softly.

She obeyed, her eyes never leaving him as he undressed. His hands went to his belt and she watched with avid interest as he undid the gold buckle. He worked the fastener next, then the zipper. With one lithe, fluid movement he divested himself of both trousers and underwear and stood over her, naked and proud and aroused.

He searched her face, looking for any sign of regret or dislike or hesitation. He hadn't felt so unsure of his own appeal since adolescence. Such modesty was unlike him. He wanted to be all she had ever desired in a man. What if she didn't like him, was repulsed by him?

But all he saw in her eyes was the shining expression of a woman waiting to be loved. He lay down and drew her under him. Their bodies adjusted to each other with the comfort of old acquaintances and the expectant excitement of a rollercoaster ride.

"I've wanted this for so long, to be lying naked with you underneath me. Tell me it feels as good to you as it does to me." Lovingly his mouth glanced over the features of her face.

Sloan's eyes closed with the pleasure of having his weight atop her. "It feels wonderful." He buried his face in the hollow between her neck and shoulder, and she stroked through the dark shaggy strands from the top of his head to his nape.

Her hands coasted over his shoulders and down the smooth planes of his back. The muscles were firm, the skin warm. The small of his back dipped vulnerably before the tautness of his buttocks reminded her just how masculine he was. The backs of his thighs were dusted with hair.

"You're so hard," she murmured in awed appreciation.

She felt his chuckle. "Um-huh."

"I didn't mean just *that*," she said with a shy smile. "I meant generally, all over."

"Thank you, but right now *that* is demanding most of my concentration." He lifted his head to brush soft kisses on her lips. He angled his body to one side of her and granted himself the privilege of taking stimulating liberties. "And by contrast, you're soft. Soft and sweet."

"Am I?" she sighed tremulously as he kissed her throat and the upper part of her chest. Her neck arched prettily and he dragged his tongue down its satiny length.

"Yes, yes," was his harsh whisper as his hand wrapped around her breast, gently squeezed it upward, and plucked at the rosy peak with his lips. "You taste so damn good, Sloan."

His tongue laved her nipple until it puckered with longing. She held her breath, clutching at his hair with both hands. When he enveloped her with his mouth, she exhaled on a low, satisfied moan. He flexed his fingers and his jaws simultaneously with a tugging she felt deep inside her womb. She called his name plaintively.

"Am I hurting you?"

"No, no." A curtain of hair swished around her face as she shook her head from side to side.

"Do you like this?" he asked, as his mouth moved to the other breast while his fingertips stayed to appease the one that was already shiny and wet from his loving.

"Carter, Carter." That fervent repetition of his name was the best way she knew to answer him. It was the only way she could answer him while she swirled in this maelstrom of desire. Her heart was spiraling upward out of her body and her brain had long since taken flight.

He wasn't merely doing something physically satisfying for her. And she wasn't allowing him to use her for his own pleasure. It was an exchange, and it was exhilarating. At the moment, her passion-blurred mind couldn't sort out her myriad emotions about what was happening. It defied classification. She only knew that it was the highest level of loving she'd ever experienced.

His hand drifted down her stomach, massaging the supple flesh. He levered himself up to look at her navel as his finger traced the fragile rim and tested its depth. He smiled as he played with it in studious delight, like a baby who has just discovered his toes.

But his eyes came back to hers when his hand lowered to the downy triangle that secreted her womanhood. Its perimeter was outlined by an adoring fingertip. Lightly he combed through the sweet nest and watched her eyes dilate with desire. Even as he watched that miracle of nature, his hand caressed its way down to press open her thighs. His touch was exquisitely tender, yet bold, confident yet humble, as he introduced his fingers into the moist protective petals.

"Sloan." His lips formed her name, but had she not been watching him, she wouldn't have heard it. A quiet purr in her throat was her only response. That and the gentle thrust of her hips against his hand as she arched her back. "So very woman." His exploration went beyond the bounds of timidity and inhibition.

Wave after wave of passion washed over her, leaving her a little more breathless each time. She felt herself melting against his heat, felt her nipples begging for surcease, felt herself losing her grip on reason as his fingers continued to stroke, to feather, to circle until she was gasping for breath.

"Carter," she cried as her flesh contracted around his fingers. His eyes glazed.

"You're killing me," he ground out as he withdrew his hand and poised himself between her thighs. "Sweet . . ." He gnashed his teeth in an exercise of self control as he bathed the spearhead of his desire with her dew. He bent down and kissed her breasts, gentle, homage-paying kisses, before he slowly let himself enter the haven she promised.

"Oh, my God," he breathed into her ear as he lay his head next to hers. Full and hard, he pulsed inside her while they tried to define for their own mystified minds the wonder of it.

"You fill me completely." Her hands roved his back, trying to draw him closer, which was impossible. She turned her head and let her lips ghost over his ear and the hair that grazed the top of it. Catching his earlobe between her teeth, she beseeched softly. "Move inside me."

He growled an assent, but his motions were tentative at first. "You're so . . . small," he anguished. "Am I hurting you?"

Her fingers curled deeper into the flesh of his hips imploringly. "No."

"I can make it better for us."

"I'm disappointing you?" she asked in sudden panic.

"No, sweetheart, no. Only listen and do as I tell you and it'll be better."

His instructions were softly spoken and his praise when she complied was loving. "You're precious," he murmured as his movements became swifter to match their accelerated passion. "Precious, Sloan, do you hear me?"

She could hear him. His voice, his rushing breath, his pounding heartbeat that echoed hers. She could hear too, their harmonizing ecstatic cries as they both lost all contact with the world.

Their descent was as sweetly loving, if not as clamorous, as the ascent had been. Her voice was drowsy, drugged with love, as she asked him, "What have you done to me, Carter Madison?"

"Loved you as you should have always been loved." He lifted his head and rained love on her from his glowing eyes. "The real question is," he whispered, "what have you done to me?"

"Should we go upstairs?" he asked into her hair. They lay face to face, her head cradled against his chest. Lazily his fingers were twining through her hair.

"No," she said, rubbing her face back and forth over the hair-matted wall of his chest. "Not just yet. This is too . . . I don't want to move." Even after he had rolled them to their sides, he remained nestled inside her. "It feels so good."

"Does it?" With an index finger under her chin he lifted her face for a gentle kiss. She trembled. "Are you cold?" He had enfolded them both in the blanket.

"No. I'm still feeling aftershocks."

Confidentially he whispered, "So am I." He stirred inside her and she ducked her head shyly.

"That was a terribly brazen thing I did. Taking off my robe that way. Asking you to make love to me."

At the time she hadn't thought about having the courage to woo him, or the right or wrong of it. She had simply obeyed her instinct and he had heeded his own. Neither regretted it. Of that she was certain.

It was wrong. Alicia had been betrayed and everything Sloan had stood for had been compromised. But she wasn't sorry for it. Alicia would have Carter for the rest of his life. Tonight, for a few brief hours, he belonged to Sloan. The consequences could be lamented later. The only worry that plagued her now was if she had disappointed him.

"I know I'm awkward." Her hand was self-consciously restless as it tweaked the hair on his chest.

"Sloan." He repeated her name until she met his eyes in the flickering firelight. "I am content. More content than I've ever been with a woman. You are what I need, more than I could ever hope for. Please don't insult me by belittling yourself. I love you, Sloan."

"I love you," she vowed as tears pooled in her

eyes, mirroring the nearby flames. "I love you so much it hurts." She tilted her head back for his kiss. His tongue entered her mouth lovingly, with a sincerity that touched her soul.

"I think that bastard you were engaged to was an insensitive fool. Didn't he ever teach you the finer techniques of loving? Wasn't it a sharing thing?"

She shook her head. "No. At least I never felt with him what I do with you."

"You've been made to feel inferior when in fact the opposite is true. You're body is beautiful, Sloan. Except for this tragic scar."

"What scar?" she asked, pushing away from him slightly.

"Right here." He trailed his finger down between her breasts. The cleavage was more pronounced because of her position and all but swallowed his finger. "That's where your heart has been broken. The scar is invisible, but I can see it. Let me heal it now, once and for all."

He dipped his head and placed his mouth on the soft, fragrant flesh of her breasts. "Don't ever let anyone hurt you again, Sloan." He kissed her with ardent lips that indeed seemed to draw all the hurt out of her. Her heart soared with newfound freedom. "You are a beautiful woman with a tremendous capacity to love. Watch me while I take away all your pain."

Raising her head, she did watch as his nose nudged against her breasts. Their lush round shape was measured, treasured, appreciated by his hands. The shadow of his dear head spread over her breasts like healing lotion.

She saw the shadow of his tongue on her nipple before she actually felt its damp, deft touch. That gentle aggressor fanned the fires of her desire which she had erroneously thought were quenched. They burst into instant life, hotter and more intense than before. Her head dropped back onto the floor as her eyes closed. She danced again the ballet she had only recently learned, a mindless undulation that responded to the drumbeats in her head and heart and loins.

"See what a priceless woman you are." She was lifted over him, his hand covering her hips and pressing, encouraging her to feel his desire that had filled her again.

"Carter, you're—"

"Yes. Slowly dying. Now it's your turn to heal me."

She awoke languidly to lips planting tiny kisses on her neck. Even before she opened her eyes, she stretched luxuriously beneath the sheets, loving the way they slid around her nakedness. She'd never slept in any bed in the house other than the one in her room. It had been a rare privilege for many reasons for Carter to carry her upstairs during the night and establish her in the bed he'd slept in alone for weeks.

Now her breast was the object of his fondling as he trailed kisses along her shoulder. "Milady's breakfast is served."

Sloan opened her eyes and they lighted on the window. It was still raining, but the steady dripping sound was welcomed. Somehow it helped assure their privacy, set them apart, separated them from the world. It also contributed to her own sensuous birth where all stimuli were magnified in her brain. Besides seeing and hearing the rain, she could smell it, taste it, feel it falling on her skin.

"What did you say?" she mumbled into the pillow, sighing. A silly smile curled her lips when his fingers found her nipple already distended and begging for his caress.

"I said, milady's breakfast is served." His mouth availed itself of what his fingers had tenderly prepared for it, sucking her nipple lightly. His finger-tips whispered down her stomach to disturb the tawny nest at the top of her thighs with flirtatious strokings.

"Ummmm," she groaned. "What is on milady's menu?" she asked insinuatingly against that carnal mouth that had made its way up to hers.

He parted her lips with an aggressive tongue and swept it possessively as though he didn't want her to entertain any notions that his ownership had ended with the approach of morning. "An omelette, English muffins, orange marmalade, crisp bacon and coffee."

Shoving him away, Sloan sat upright in the bed, disregarding the sheet that settled around her waist. As he enumerated the breakfast dishes, she realized that those were the tantalizing aromas she could smell. She spotted the laden silver tray at the foot of the bed and cried out in surprise.

"You really are serving me breakfast in bed!"

He wasn't looking at the tray and was paying scant attention to her surprise. Rather, he was scrutinizing her breasts, blushing with sleep and sex, and so provocatively displayed for him. He rode their sloping shape with an indolent finger. "After the way you served me last night, I thought it was the least I could do."

"Oh!" she exclaimed, grabbing his finger, bending it back to a torturous angle and saying, "Just as I thought. You don't respect me in the morning."

He pounced on her, tossing her back amidst the pillows and pinioning her naked body beneath his that was unfairly fully clothed. He ravaged her mouth with a playfully savage kiss. "It's my respect you want, huh?"

Primly she answered, "On an empty stomach, yes."

"And after breakfast?"

She lowered her lashes in a demure way that delighted him because he could see the lasciviousness of her thoughts twinkling behind the mask of false modesty. "That's for milord to wait and find out," she teased throatily.

They demolished the food on the tray. "This is delicious," she said, taking another bite of the cheesy omelette. "But I still don't think it's right that you did it. *I'm* supposed to be the hostess, remember?"

"You deserve to be indulged. And you'd better wait before you thank me too profusely."

"Why?" she asked warily, her fork poised in front of her mouth. He avoided answering by sipping his coffee. "Carter?"

"I don't clean as I go."

She set her fork down. "You're telling me that my kitchen is a disaster, right?"

"I wouldn't go so far as to say *disaster*."

She crossed her arms under her breasts and tried to look stern, an expression that looked incongruous considering her bobbing breasts and her beguilingly disarrayed hair. Carter had a hard time keeping a straight face as she demanded. "How far would you go?"

He squinted his eyes. "Uh . . . shambles. Yeah, that's the right word. Your kitchen is in shambles."

"What's the use of having breakfast served to you in bed if you have to worry about cleaning up a shambles?"

"I guess I'll have to find a way of making it up to you," he drawled, lifting the tray from the bed.

He had a most persuasive way of taking her mind off the kitchen. It started in the shower where he soaped her body, massaging her flesh between his lathered fingers. She insisted on washing his hair and he sat on the tile bench while she worked shampoo into the thick strands. They stood together under the spray, letting the water sluice down their bodies, following the runnels with eyes and hands and lips until they fell on each other in a tempestuous kiss.

Sloan was already reclining against the pillows when he came out of the bathroom vigorously drying his hair with a towel. She watched the lithe movements of his muscles. As she had noted the first time she saw him, no motions were wasted. He was lean and sinewy, with a lethal sleekness about him that reminded her of the heroes in his books. He wasn't musclebound, yet there was about him a sense of ruthlessness lurking just below the surface. It excited her.

He dropped the towel on the floor and stepped over it negligently, looking down at her where she lay with sultry perfection on the linens. He didn't move as she reached up and took his hand.

"You're very nice to look at, Mr. Madison." Her voice held the mellow seductiveness of a silk scarf being pulled over harp strings.

"I have knobby knees."

"They are *not* knobby," she said in fierce defense of her lover. When his brow arched skeptically she assessed his knees more closely, smiled, and said more softly, "Well, not too knobby."

The role of aggressor became hers as she pulled him down onto the bed. Delighted with her brave interest, he submitted to her silent directives and lay down on his back. Her touch was timorous as she began to examine him curiously.

"I'm shy of you, Carter. Of your nakedness."

"I know," he said softly. "Don't be. I don't ever want you to be afraid to touch me."

He wouldn't have been surprised last night to discover she was a virgin. It had been apparent from the first that her skills were limited. But there had been no doubt as to her passion. The way she'd stood before him naked and boldly proclaiming her need had made his heart fill with pride that she'd finally recognized herself as a sexual woman.

Her fevered movements against him had been hungry and wild and he'd loved it. But he saw in her no coy demonstrations of desire, no affected sounds of mounting passion, no rehearsed caresses. She'd been totally honest, almost innocent in her passion, and God, that alone had been enough to make him love her with a ferocity that frightened him. Compared to her, all the other women he'd ever known seemed like animated mannequins who had performed for him as they thought he wanted them to.

But hadn't he, too, always performed? Hadn't his sighs and loving words been little more than scripted, often lifted out of the pages of his own books? Hadn't he recited the words he knew they would want to hear only so he could bring them to a quick lusty climax and be done with it? And hadn't the emptiness inside him afterward often been more than he could stomach? Hadn't he felt physically purged, but spiritually sullied?

Not so last night. He'd known the moment he felt her moist tightness glove him that Sloan was unique. This was what it was to love, not *make* something, but to let it happen. Sex had ceased to be a bodily function and had become an exercise of the spirit, a blending of two whole personalities and not just a meaningless, temporary fusion of the flesh.

He had loved teaching her the subtleties of it, the rapture in detention, the pleasure in finesse. And he'd wanted to kill that bastard who had cheated her out of it before. Yet that wasn't quite the truth. If Jason had loved her the way she should have been loved, she wouldn't belong to him now. He wouldn't have had the privilege of leading her into a realm of ecstasy she'd never known existed.

Now she was kneeling over him, bashfully learning his body. And he wondered how in God's name he was ever going to give her up.

She looked at him and smiled when her finger circled a prominent patella. "Not so knobby," she whispered. His thigh muscles flexed spasmodically as her hands crept up them. He held his breath when they reached the juncture where his arousal was already becoming apparent. He didn't breathe again until her attention wandered to his navel.

Before he could quite prepare himself for it, she leaned down and kissed the hair-whorled dimple fleetingly. His clenching fingers tangled in her hair, still damp from their romp in the shower. "Ahhhh, Sloan."

Praise made her courageous. Her tongue raked his navel roughly, then dipped into it in shallow forays that robbed him of breath.

She pressed her breasts against the rigid column of his thigh as she bent over him. Her hand meandered with seeming aimlessness down his torso until it encountered the thick bush of dark hair. She tested its texture against her lips as she whispered, "I love you," and unselfishly she showed him her love until he could stand no more.

He lifted her, pressed her into the pillows, and buried himself in the feminine arbor made wet with love for him. "You are mine, Sloan. No matter what happens, I want you to know that I've never loved like I do at this moment. Feel my love, take it. Please. God, please. Take it, Sloan."

"Yes, yes," she sobbed, wrapping herself around him.

Her name became a reverent chant in her ear as he patiently contained himself until she, too, had reached the summit. When he showered her womb with life, it was a rebirth for them both.

Over her strenuous objections, he helped her restore the kitchen. They were ostensibly washing dishes, though their hands were mating in the sudsy water and their lips were sealed over the steamy sink when the telephone rang.

"Don't answer," he grumbled.

"I have to. It may be someone wanting to book all six rooms for next week."

"You'll only have five available. Unless you share yours with me," he called as she raced for the extention in her room.

"Hi. Is Mr. Madison there?" an immature voice piped.

"Yes. Who's calling please?" She clutched the receiver because she knew who the caller was and felt guilt and depression as heavy as iron chains winding around her.

"David Russell."

She squeezed her eyes shut and stifled a sob. "H—Hello, David. This is Sloan. You remember me, don't you?"

"Sure. My mom talks about you all the time. Do you have blond hair?"

"Yes. Sort of blond."

"Yeah, I remember. Can I talk to Carter now? It's important."

"There's nothing wrong, is there? With your mom or Adam?"

"No. My mom's not here. I'm at Grandma's house. But she gave me permission to call."

"Just a minute." She held the receiver to her chest, taking great breaths and trying to fend off the waves of despair that threatened to drown her. When at last she turned around to call Carter, he was standing in the doorway, a dishtowel thrown over one shoulder, watching her. A severe grimness had thinned his lips and she remembered thinking of that latent strain of violence in him.

Silently he reached for the phone, and listlessly, she handed it to him. When she tried to move past him, he manacled her wrist and sat down on the bed, pulling her onto his lap. She struggled, but to no avail. He held her there, his eyes boring into her chalky face as he brought the receiver to his ear.

"Hello," he said emotionlessly. He showed a bit more animation when he said, "Hi, buddy. How's your brother? . . . Well I miss you, too, but you knew I had to come here to work. . . . What is it that Adam's doing? . . . Well you're the oldest and you need to set a good example. . . . No, it's not fair, but few things are."

Sloan hazarded a glance at him and saw that the last had been addressed to her, not the telephone. His eyes begged for her tolerance, not understanding, not forgiveness, only tolerance of an intolerable situation.

"Tell you what, you ask Adam not to pull hair and you don't worry your grandmother with tattling on him. I'll have a talk with Adam when I get back. Okay? . . . Yeah, I can't wait either. . . . You bet. *Two* ice cream cones. Good-bye."

Without releasing her, he replaced the telephone. For long, silent moments she sat stonily on his lap. Finally she said, "Please let me go."

"I can't," he said through gritted teeth. He wasn't talking about physically releasing her right then, he was referring to the time when they'd have to part permanently.

She didn't pretend to misunderstand. "You'll have to," she sobbed, trying futilely to tear herself from his grip on her upper arms.

"But not today. Not now." He burrowed his face between her breasts that were full and unfettered beneath her blouse. His head rutted against her like a child seeking solace, peace, sustenance. "Please don't deny me you, Sloan. I *need* you. Please."

Mindless of anything save his heartfelt plea, she flung her arms around his head and clutched it to her bosom. Covering the top of his head with frantic, random kisses, she echoed his words. "I need you. I was dying until you."

They were hampered but slightly by their clothing. They tore at it, groped and grappled until they were free enough to unite in a scalding, swift possession. All their frustration, anguish, fear went into each fierce thrust. They were on a timetable and the clock was running out. They raced against it. Wanting to banish the world, to rid themselves of conscience, to hold onto their shrinking piece of heaven, they ground together. The ablution came from Carter, a warm, sweet bath that cleansed them of their torment.

Afterwards, his hair clinging damply to her skin as he rested his head heavily on her breasts, he said, "Sloan, now I can write the final love scene."

Chapter Eight

For the rest of the afternoon and into the evening he worked with total absorption. Sloan checked on him periodically, sometimes taking him a fresh cup of coffee or a cold drink, sometimes just standing at the door of his room and silently watching as he deliberated over the words he was immortalizing on paper.

Since their breakfast had been so plentiful and eaten late, she fixed him "finger food" for a light supper. She cut two sandwiches in quarters and surrounded them on the platter with sliced fruit and raw vegetables. When she carried the tray into the room, he was staring at the sheet of paper rolled into his tyepwriter, his elbows spread wide on either side of the keyboard, his chin propped on his clasped hands. His glasses, for once, were in their proper place.

She sat the tray on the table as unobtrusively as she could and turned to tiptoe out. He caught her wrist as she went by and brought her hand to his mouth, planting a quick kiss in its palm. "Thanks, love," he said absently. His eyes never left the page. Somehow that distracted, automatic show of affection meant more to her then than a long, lingering embrace would have. He had taken it for granted that she would feel his love even if he was concentrating on his work.

She busied herself with unnecessary tasks downstairs, baked a few dozen cookies, and then undressed and got herself ready for bed. She made one last trip up the stairs to take him a plate of cookies and a thermal carafe of coffee. He was still at it, bent over a sheet of manuscript, mercilessly slashing it with his red ink pen. All the food on the other tray had been eaten. She moved it aside and put the plate of cookies in its place.

His head came up and he focused on her. "What is that heavenly smell?"

"Chocolate chip cookies."

"I'm not talking about the cookies," he said, bringing her around to the side of his chair. "I'm talking about you." Drawing her close, he parted her robe and lay his head against her stomach. "You always smell so good," he mumbled contentedly, yawning broadly.

She ruffled through his hair that she guessed had been abused by aggravated fingers. "Are you tired?"

"Getting that way. But I need to work a while longer."

"Eat some cookies. The coffee in the thermos is fresh and hot." Her words came out on short gusts of air. He was sliding his face over her silky nightgown, nuzzling her stomach and abdomen with his nose and chin. Occasionally his lips would open, and she would feel the warm vapor of his breath filtering through the sheer garment to tantalize her skin.

"So am I. Fresh and hot, that is," he snarled against the indentation of her navel.

Taking handfuls of hair in her fists, she forced his head up and said scoldingly. "But you have to work."

"Slavedriver," he grumbled.

Leaning down, she kissed him chastely on the mouth. "Good night." She turned to leave, but he caught the hem of her robe and jerked her to a halt.

"Just where do you think you're going?"

"Downstairs to bed."

"Wrong. To bed. Over there." He nodded toward the bed they had shared the night before.

"But you have to work, Carter."

"I'll work. You'll sleep. If I won't disturb you."

"That's not the point. *I'll* disturb you."

He shook his head. "No you won't. Please stay in the room with me."

She looked at him out of the corner of her eye. "Are you sure?"

"Positive. I want you with me."

"Okay, I'll take this tray downstairs and bring a book up with me. But if I see that I'm distracting you, I'll leave."

"Deal."

He was true to his word. When she came back, he was struggling with another phrase, muttering it repetitiously under his breath. She switched on the bedside table lamp and slid between the sheets. Picking up her Carter Madison novel, she adjusted it on her lap, propped herself on the pillows, and began to read. Two hours later, engrossing as the story was, she couldn't suppress her yawns and finally surrendered to sleepiness. Carter was still poring over the pages he'd typed. She fell asleep listening to the tapping keys of the typewriter and marveling over his self-discipline.

The sinking of the mattress awakened her a moment before she was cradled against his lean, naked body. "Carter?"

"It had better be," he chuckled.

"Are you finished?"

"You're so warm." He snuggled against her, finding the soft warmth of her neck with searching lips. His hands closed around her waist.

"Aren't you tired?" she asked on a yawn.

"Exhausted. What does this do?" One hand was blindly struggling with the neckline of her nightgown.

"It unties."

"Ah, there," he said, gratified when the cord loosened and fell away. He moved down her body, kissing the upper curves of her breasts. Suddenly he raised his head. "I'm sorry, Sloan. I'm a selfish beast to wake you up in the middle of the night like this."

"Yes, you're beastly," she sighed. After lowering the nightgown herself, she found his hand in the darkness and lay it on her breast. With slow circular motions she moved his hand until her nipple grew ripe in his palm. "Look what you've done to me, you beast."

His whispered words were somewhere between blasphemy and prayer. While his hand continued to fondle her breast and its responsive crown, his lips melded into hers. His tongue delved deeply, then withdrew to match hers in a darting, thrusting, rubbing skirmish. He sampled the skin of her throat and chest and shoulders with lovebites. His kisses were hot, damp, increasing the fever that suffused her flesh with a rosy glow.

Cherishing her, he peeled the nightgown away from her other breast and feasted his eyes on the erogenous display. The nipples were taut and dark from his caressing fingers. The mounds rose gently from her chest like offerings on an altar of love. And he was the high priest.

His mouth covered her with a sweet suction

and drew on her nipple with tender hunger. He loved her thoroughly, his tongue honoring her with delicate strokes, his mouth closing around her as though to take all of her sweetness into himself.

Not only her consciousness was awake now, but every cell in her body was clamoring for his. She writhed against him, twisting the nightgown and trying to kick it free with thrashing legs. He helped, shoving the garment down as his hand smoothed along the top of her thighs, in between, possessing her womanhood with a cupping, loving hand. Gently she was explored, tantalized, coaxed to a raging passion that threatened to ignite her.

Inch by alluring inch he eased down her body, at last totally freeing her of the nightgown. Letting her legs drape the sides of his body, he kissed her navel with the same talent as he kissed her mouth. His lips sipped at it, his tongue flicking into the small crevice as though it were a precious receptacle containing rare nectar.

His breath disturbed the golden tangle of curls on the slight mound and she cried out his name in astonishment and not a little fear. "No, Carter."

"I love you, Sloan. I want to experience all of you."

His adoration was bold and gentle, carnal and holy. She felt not the least bit violated, but a great deal embellished by the sweep of his lips and the thrust of his tongue. His loving was so exquisite that she was cocooned by bliss. When the crisis came, she called his name. He was there, crushing her to him, involving himself in the magic of her and enriching it with his essence.

Thoroughly spent, he rolled them to their sides. She lay like a doll against his chest, her arms and legs sprawled limply over his. His hands smoothed her back, the swell of her hips, the length of her thighs.

"I can't believe I've lived this long without having your love," she whispered weakly.

"You have had it. I've always loved you," he said quietly, threading his fingers through her hair to press her head against his heart. "I just never knew your name."

He was sitting on the edge of the bed watching her when she opened her eyes the next morning. He was wearing only his underwear, which did more to detail his sex than to cover it. Without speaking he handed her the crumpled, ink-scarred pages of his manuscript.

She looked at him inquiringly, then at the pages offered her. Taking them, she sat up in bed, discreetly pulling the sheet over her chest. He smiled before he stood and went to the window where a watery sun was peeking through the clouds.

Line after line of the manuscript was gobbled up by her avaricious eyes. With each one, she felt another door of her soul opening up. It wasn't Gregory and Lisa living on the pages. It was she and Carter, loving without restraint, expressing their love not only with their bodies, but with their sensitivity for the other's needs. When she had read the last line, she lowered the page and with tear-filled eyes met his across the room.

"It's us, isn't it?"

He left the window and came to sit down beside her. His shaking fingers brushed back tousled strands of hair from her cheek. "Yes."

"When did you finish it?"

"Just now. I worked on it after you had gone to sleep . . . the second time. I couldn't get the love sequence right until . . . until you." His smile was half-hearted. She could see tears glossing his own eyes.

"This isn't the ending." It wasn't a question.

"I can't write the ending, Sloan."

"But you know what it will be."

"We both know what it will be."

"Yes," she said, laying her cheek in his palm and shutting her eyes. "We've always known he'll have to leave her."

"But in the meantime, they'll love each other without any regrets, as though there were no future, as though each day were an eternity unto itself."

She smiled at him tremulously. "Yes," she said softly, then repeated it with more emphasis. "Yes, yes." Clasping his face between her hands she kissed him, telling him of her love with softly parted lips and a prowling tongue. "Why don't you sleep for a while and I'll bring you your breakfast later."

"On one condition. You stay with me until I'm asleep."

For an answer, she raised the covers and let him slide in beside her. Fitting her body into the curve of his, he fell asleep in a matter of minutes. He didn't awaken when she got up, but there was a peaceful smile on his rugged face.

The days passed far too quickly and they tried not to mark the limited hours allowed them. They lived vagariously according to their appetites, their moods, their libidos. Carter had the lecherous idea of enshrining every bedroom in the house in a most appropriate way. Sloan refused, reminding him of all the linens she would have to wash and iron. His creative mind came into play and she relented to his wishes, amazed by how inventive he could be.

As she sat facing him, her legs straddling his, on the rug on one of the bedroom floors, she watched the effect of her loveplay on his nipples. "If I read this in one of your books, I'm going to know I inspired the scene."

He tilted her head up to meet his heated gaze. "Didn't you know that from now on, you *are* my inspiration." He moved deeper into her in a way that left his meaning crystal clear.

The rain, which had been everyone else's nemesis and their blessing, abated. The sun, after a few days of maidenly coyness, bared herself to the pale San Franciscans.

Sloan rebooked three rooms that had been previously cancelled. The guests were due to arrive the following week. She made more reservations for coming months and thought that with just a little luck, she might recoup the losses the unnaturally disagreeable weather had cost her.

"Hey, hey, what do you know? A bookstore!" Carter chortled. They had gone out to replenish her pantry and to soak up some sunshine. After storing her packages in the car, they had decided to walk and window shop for the sake of needed exercise. Carter now caught her arm and dragged her toward the door of the old house near Washington Square that had been quaintly converted into a two-level bookstore.

The bell over the door tinkled pleasantly as they went in. The musty proprietor peered at them over the top of his half-glasses and nodded a greeting with his bald head, then went back to his book.

"He didn't recognize you," Sloan whispered as Carter led her toward the racks of fiction.

"They usually don't. I don't mind as long as they sell my books."

"It's that dreadful picture on the dust jacket."

"How would you have me photographed?"

She hauled his head down and whispered her lewd suggestion in his ear. The whimsical eyebrow scowled in feigned disbelief. "You're a wanton broad. Did you know that?"

"Only recently."

"Well, you're in luck." He grabbed an appreciable

handful of jean-covered fanny and squeezed it. "I have a lech for wanton broads."

She squirmed away and glanced nervously over her shoulder at the bookseller, who thankfully was still immersed in the pages of his book. "Yes, I know, Mr. Madison. I've read your books," she hissed.

"Wait until you read the next one. It's going to have a bathtub scene you won't believe."

"Carter!" she exclaimed, putting her hands on her hips and drawing her sweater tight across braless breasts. He had selected her wardrobe that morning. "You promised not to write about that!" Her cheeks blushed most becomingly.

"I did?"

"Yes!"

"I only promised that to get you to participate," he said with an unrepentant shrug. "You're great at orgies. And don't get all huffy because you know you loved it just as much as I did. Let's see now," he said, ignoring her indignant look and perusing the shelves. "J, k, l, l-a, l-o, L-u, Ludlum. God, I wish he'd change his name. His books are always shelved just above mine. Ah, here we are, Carter Madison."

"How many Carter Madison novels are there?" she asked, already having forgiven him.

"Twelve. And this marvelous bookstore with excellent taste has all of them in stock. *Sleeping Mistress* will be thirteen. I hope that's not unlucky."

"All twelve are best sellers?"

"Not the first two. The others, yes."

"How many movies?"

"Two. And one television series. The credit reads, 'Based on a novel by Carter Madison.' "

She pondered his wrinkled forehead. "The fame and fortune make you uneasy, don't they?" Her intuition was founded on love.

His sherry-colored eyes sought hers and held them. "A bit, yes."

"Why, Carter?"

He sighed and leaned against the shelf, taking her hand and studying it as he answered slowly. "I don't know. Sometimes I feel like a well-paid whore."

"That's ridiculous!"

"Is it? My writing is technically correct, my style is my own, not a bastardization of someone else's, I do what I do well, I bring pleasure. But sometimes I feel like what I've done is meaningless. A parody of the real thing. I had such aspirations and goals when I began and none of them related to money."

"Money's the barometer by which the world measures success. Just because you're paid a lot of it, doesn't conversely reduce the value of your writing."

"I suppose so," he said with a rueful smile. "Still I'd like to do a truly meaningful novel whether it was a commercial success or not."

"Why don't you then?"

His eyes whipped up from her hand to her face. It was as though no one had ever challenged him to it before. "Do you think I could?"

"I know you could. You've got the talent. Your writing is superb. Just direct it in the channel you want it to go. Please yourself with the book you want to write. I assume you already have a plot in mind?"

"Yes." He nodded excitedly.

"Okay. Write the book you want to do and then go back to writing what the public wants. At least you'll have satisfied yourself. And I can't really imagine the public scorning *any* Carter Madison book, especially one as marvelous as that one is bound to be."

He studied her quietly for a long moment, his finger stroking her cheek. She could feel the love emanating from him and seeping into her. "You're something," he mouthed.

"*You're* something," she responded in kind.

"I love you so much."

"I love you."

He scooted closer. "I can see you, imagine you rather, under your sweater. Do you think our studious proprietor would notice if we slipped into his storeroom and I—"

"Well, well, well, there's a celebrity in our midst."

The voice was snide and deprecating, having been filtered through a pinched, sanctimonious nose.

The man who had intruded on their privacy was slight, several inches shorter than Sloan. His hair was clipped close to his scalp and only brought attention to the narrowness of his head. A sharply pointed goatee gave him a sinister aspect. His eyes were as shifty and busy as a ferret's. His clothes were natty. A turtleneck sweater was anchored to his chest by ropes of gold chains.

"You're far too humble, Sydney," Carter drawled, edging closer to Sloan in what she sensed was a protective gesture. "You're as much a celebrity as I."

"A celebrity perhaps. Humble? Not at all, Mr. Madison. I consider my opinions to be sterling, as do my readers."

Sloan could feel Carter's muscles bunching with angry tension. "Ms. Sloan Fairchild, Mr. Sydney Gladstone." He made the introduction out of necessity and with as little flair as possible.

"Hello, Mr. Gladstone," she murmured, not daring to offer her hand, afraid Carter would snatch it back like a mother keeping her child away from a snake.

"Ms. Fairchild," Gladstone oozed, executing a jerky little bow.

She knew who the man was. His column was run twice a week in the book section of the *Chronicle* and she knew it was syndicated to other major newspapers. She didn't read him. She found his columns to be petty and vindictive, almost always taking pot shots at the writers rather than addressing what they'd written. It was all she could do to keep from shivering as his cunning eyes toured her with lurid interest.

"We didn't hear you come in," Carter said.

He laughed, and it was a nasty, decayed sound. "Implying that you would have taken your leave sooner if you had. Really, Mr. Madison, are you still piqued by my critique in *Publisher's Weekly* of your last book?"

"I wasn't piqued. Nor am I now. It, like all your articles, was tripe."

The skinny nostrils almost closed in vexation. "Nevertheless I see you took my advice." He eyed Sloan again in a way that made her feel like she needed a bath.

"What advice was that, Sydney?" Carter crossed his arms over his chest and put all his weight on one foot in an attitude of extreme boredom. Sloan wasn't fooled. If Gladstone weren't a complete fool, he wouldn't be either.

"If you'll recall I said that the love sequences in your novels were predictable and lackluster."

"If that means my characters aren't into group sex, bedroom gymnastics, perversions, whips and chains, etc., etc., you're right and I'm flattered."

The critic sniffed fastidiously. "That's not entirely what I meant. I think your sexual passages lack a certain excitement, depth. What I said in the critique was that your fictional love affairs had become staid, emotionless, and trite. I suggested that your readers might benefit from your getting a new love interest of your own." He slanted a crude glance at Sloan. "I see by the way you could barely keep your hands from under Ms. Fairchild's sweater that you've taken my advice."

Carter's arms dropped to his sides as he balled his hands into fists. "You sonofabitch."

"Save your gutter language for your heroes, Mr. Madison. It suits them perfectly. And I despise violence when it doesn't reside on the pages of a book so spare me your growls and feral looks. I personally am delighted that you've found a new source of inspiration. I was rather dreading *Sleeping Mistress*." His eyes cemented on Sloan's breasts. "Now I'm rather looking forward to each page," he said with a noticeable slur. "Though I doubt you let a mistress like Ms. Fairchild sleep very often."

Carter was at his throat in one lunge. The man was slammed into the bookshelf with his Adam's apple the victim of Carter's steely fingers. "You listen and you listen good, Sydney. I'd dearly love to strangle you with one of your pretty necklaces, but you're not worth the effort. Your columns are crocks of crap and anyone who reads them knows that. How the hell you think you know anything about loving a woman, I don't know. The only lust you've ever felt is when you're raking some undeserving author over the coals. And if that's the only way you can get your jollies, I pity you.

"But for what you said about Ms. Fairchild, I could easily kill you. And if you print one word about her, even insinuate anything about her, I'll come after you. I'll make it my business to see if there's anything to you to castrate. And if there is—"

"What's the trouble back there?"

The proprietor had finally been roused from his book.

"No trouble," Carter called back. Only then did he release the sagging, choking critic from his deathgrip. He wasn't done yet. His eyes and his voice slashed across Gladstone's face. "You remember what I said," was his deadly warning before he gently took Sloan's arm and led her from the store.

How her knees supported her until they reached the car, she never knew. Carter ushered her into the passenger side with tender courtesy. "God I'm sorry, Sloan," he said when he got in.

"It wasn't your fault."

"No but it was my grudge match. I called him a pompous, no-talent ass on the *Tonight Show* once and he can't quite find it in himself to forgive me."

His attempt at humor failed miserably. She continued to stare out the windshield in a daze. The white stillness of her face caused alarm to worm through his entrails, but there was nothing he could do about it parked in a car on a public street. He crammed the car into first gear, lurched into traffic and made record time getting them to Fairchild House. Wordlessly he helped her carry in her packages and deposited them on the kitchen table.

He reached for her. "Sloan—"

"No!"

He was stunned as she dodged his embrace. He could feel his temperature dropping, his body turning cold, the fire in his soul being extinguished even as he tried desperately to keep one life-giving flame flickering.

"You can't let some bitchy, small-minded jerk like that bother you, Sloan. You're more intelligent than that. I know you are. Dammit, tell me you are!" By the time he finished, he was shouting at her in frustrated anger.

"No, no," she yelled back. "It wasn't him, it's . . ."

"What?" he demanded.

"It's *me*. What he said woke me up to the fact that I'll never be anything to you but a mistress. Oh, God. I hate that word."

"So do I. Don't ever say it again in relation to yourself."

"Why not?" she flared. "That's what I've been to you, isn't it? Not your wife. Certainly more than a friend. What would you call me?"

"Beloved," he said in a voice striving for calmness. "The woman I love."

"But not the woman you'll marry. Not the woman

you'll give your name to. Not the woman who'll share your life, have your children."

"You knew that, Sloan. We both did. And we both know that there wasn't one damn thing we could do about it. You said you'd love me while you could."

"I know," she sobbed, wringing her hands. "I thought it would be enough. It's not. I've betrayed my best friend with you. Betrayed myself. I couldn't abide having that hideous man looking at me that way, saying those things. He and everyone else will see our love as something sleazy. What's between us may be pure, but the rest of the world won't see it that way."

"Screw the rest of the world!" he shouted. "Who the hell is going to know? To care? I assure you Gladstone hasn't got the balls to print a word about you, not after what I said to him. He's all hot air and basically a coward. And even if the rest of the world did know, what would you care if what we feel for each other is honest?"

"It's *not* honest, Carter. Our love is based on deceit." She paused to draw in several deep breaths, garnering her strength and courage to do what she had to do. "You've got to leave, Carter. You can't stay here any longer."

"I can't leave you, Sloan. Not ever."

She looked at him with mingled incredulity and fury. "Surely, *surely*, you didn't intend to continue seeing me after you married Alicia," she said on a dwindling gust of air.

His failure to meet her eyes and the defensive way he shoved his hands in his pockets was as good as a confession. "No. I don't know. I can't give you up, Sloan."

"Why?" she sneered, "Because I provide you with such a great time?"

He spun around and nailed her to the floor with outraged eyes. "That's a helluva thing to say."

"Oh, I don't know," she said loftily. "Mr. Gladstone might not have been far off the mark. I'm certainly convenient. No attachments. Now that you're going to be a married family man, you can't live the flamboyant life of a wealthy bachelor. Your romantic escapades will have to be on the hush-hush. Secretive, furtive, clandestine.

"And you know, because I've ill-advisedly poured out my soul to you on more than one occasion, that I've been a doormat for everyone all my life. My parents could look right through me. Jason used me for as long as it pleased him. Now you want to run up here, no doubt with the full, un-derstanding endorsement of your loving wife, and use me whenever you need inspiration." The last word was spat at him.

His eyes dropped to the middle of her body with a crude implication. "Let you sharpen my quill, so to speak."

The moment he raised his eyes to her shattered features, he was steeped in self-hate. His expletive echoed off the ceiling as he tossed his head up-ward and then dropped his chin to his chest, trying to find some manner in which to eradicate the harmful words they'd flung at each other.

"I'm sorry, Sloan," he said at long last. Even to his own ears the words sounded hollow and dead.

"No, don't be," she said, laughing bitterly. "You are most succinct. It took you only a few words to express exactly what I had been trying to say. We have, however, come to a perfect understanding. All that could be said has been. I think you should leave. Now."

"Dammit, Sloan, you can't mean that."

"Oh, but I do," she said with indisputable resolution.

His eyes beamed into hers incisively. "You're actually going to crawl behind that goddamn shell again, aren't you? Put yourself behind that protec-tive shield of yours that's as tough as armor and just as impenetrable."

"Analysis isn't your forte, Mr. Madison. Stick to nouns and verbs and crude language and vulgar innuendos. You're very good at them."

"Begging isn't my forte either." He went to the kitchen door and pushed it open. "All right, Sloan, go back to your safe, lonely world and wallow in your selflessness. And when you try to sleep alone at night, count up all the rewards you have from it."

She watched him almost tear the door off its hinges as he pushed through it. She watched, too, as it swung back and forth until it came to a standstill, just as surely as her heart had stopped.

Chapter Nine

He was gone.

She didn't know how long she sat at the kitchen table staring vacantly into space. Twilight crept around the window sills and faded into darkness and still she sat unmoving. At one precise moment, she knew with stark clarity that he had left, that she was alone in the house. He had made no sound as he left. He had exited her life with no more fanfare than he had entered it.

Sloan forced herself to her feet and drifted through the dark hallways and up the stairs as one following a hypnotic command. The door to his room was ajar.

The emptiness was ominous. The table in the middle of the room looked like a carcass picked clean. Gone were the papers and the typewriter, his dictionary and thesaurus, his red ink pens. The floor was mournfully free of balled pieces of manuscript that had known his wrath and impatience with himself. The bathroom was clear of his personal effects; the closet stood empty beyond its gaping door. The bed was unmade. Its covers were clinging to it like the petals of a flower that had known full bloom and were now wilting and dying.

Sloan toured the room like a flagellant at a shrine, her eyes filling and flooding. Spying the sheets of unused manuscript in the wastepaper basket, she knelt, picked up each one, smoothed it out and made of them a neat stack. Pressing it to her breasts, she went to the door. She couldn't bring herself to clean the room just yet. Later, when she was stronger, she would prepare it for another's use. But not now. Not while her heart was bleeding.

Taking only the pages of words he had so carefully composed and then so easily discarded, she left the room, closing the door quietly behind her.

"Fairchild House," she said into the telephone two days later.

"Sloan."

The voice was so familiar yet so unlike itself. "Alicia?" *My God, no*! was Sloan's first thought. Something had happened to Carter. Why else would Alicia sound so forlorn? "Alicia," she repeated, gripping the receiver with a suddenly slippery hand, "what's wrong?"

"Nothing," she said dully. "At least not an emergency. I didn't mean to frighten you."

Sloan's heart returned to her chest, but the foreboding stayed like a bad taste in her mouth. "Y—you don't sound like yourself."

"For a very good reason."

Sloan mashed her fingers to colorless lips. She couldn't know! She couldn't have found out! Carter? No, he'd never . . . Sydney Gladstone! Had he written? . . . No, she'd been reading his columns. How could Alicia have found out?

"Can we talk about it?" Sloan said tearfully.

"Oh, Sloan, please, yes. I've got to talk to somebody." Alicia collapsed into tears.

Sloan was dismayed by this turn of events. Alicia wasn't referring to her affair with Carter, but to something else entirely. She was relieved, yet instantly concerned. "What is it?" she asked anxiously. "Alicia, please don't cry like that. Tell me."

"I can't. I want to, but . . . I've got to talk to somebody," she repeated.

Sloan bit her lower lip before saying. "Carter. Why don't you talk to him?"

"Carter's not here."

"Not *there*?"

"Didn't he tell you where he was going when he left Fairchild House? He didn't come to Los Angeles. He telephoned me from the airport saying he was going to New York to deliver his manuscript in person. He said he couldn't wait to unload it and that he wanted to get all the business taken care of before the wedding. It's next week, you know."

Sloan's heart felt like a lead weight in her chest, dragging her down into an abyss from which there was no escape. No doubt he hated his book now because it was a reminder of her. He couldn't wait to get rid of it, wanted to be free of it like a scab to a sore that had been a long time in crusting over. "N—no," she croaked. Clearing her throat, she said more crisply, "No, he just left one evening. He didn't say where he was going and I assumed he was going home."

"I assumed he would too, the minute he finished his book, but it's just as well under the circumstances that he didn't."

"What circumstances?" Sloan asked, getting back to the original reason for Alicia's call.

"Sloan, can you come to Los Angeles?"

Sloan coughed a short laugh. "Of course not. What are you talking about?"

"Please, Sloan. If you've ever loved me as a friend,

come down here. Just for a day. I desperately need to talk to you."

"I can't, Alicia. You can talk to me over the telephone." Sloan wished Alicia hadn't brought up that about loving her as a friend. Judas had been an exemplary friend compared to her.

"You've got to." Sloan heard the telltale huskiness in Alicia's voice again. She was crying. "I'd come up there, only I've left the boys too much recently. I'll pay for your ticket. I'll do anything, only please come, Sloan. You don't have anyone at Fairchild House now, do you? Please."

Sloan studied the brass paperweight on her desk. The desperation in Alicia's voice was genuine. Something was terribly wrong and she was reaching out to her best friend for help. If only she knew how wretched her best friend was, she would reconsider, but as it was, she thought that she needed Sloan. Sloan had already let her down once in a way that, hopefully, she'd never know. Could she refuse to help her now? Didn't she owe Alicia more than she'd ever be able to repay?

"I have guests coming next Wednesday. I'll have to come before then."

"Tomorrow," Alicia said rapidly. "Tomorrow, please."

Sloan rubbed her aching forehead with agitated fingers. Could she *ever* face Alicia? "I suppose I could. I'll catch an early plane and take a cab to your house."

"I'll be at Carter's beach house. He asked me to go over and check on things and the kids want to play on the beach."

God, would this torment, this nightmare ever end? Carter's house! "What's the address?" she asked glumly. Refusing Alicia's offer to purchase her ticket, she promised to see her the following day.

Like a sleepwalker, she lived through the rest of the day. That's how she'd moved since Carter's departure. She had lived out of habit, sleeping, waking, eating, working in the house like a programmed robot. What joy Fairchild House had previously brought her had now been altered by Carter's brief residence. Forever that large room in the corner of the second floor would be Carter's room. No amount of cleansers or vacuuming or air fresheners would rid it of him. Just as her heart would never be exorcised of his spirit.

At least she wasn't having to fret over lost revenue. Each day she was booking room reservations. If they kept coming in at the rate they had been, she'd have enough money to tide her over, and enough left to place ads in travel magazines. The future of Fairchild House depended on publicizing it. She was confident of the product she had to offer once people heard about it.

Things would work out. She'd live through this crisis just as she had survived other disappointments. Eventually it wouldn't hurt so much. His image would fade from her mind. Maybe a few successive nights would go by when she wouldn't read those pages locked away in a japanned box on her dresser. There would eventually come a time when she'd no longer remember how it felt to be held in his strong arms, the splendor of his loving.

The recovery would be slow, but she'd live.

She suffered a major setback when she stepped out of the airport taxi and saw his house outlined against a backdrop of sea and sky. It so reflected the nature of the man that her eyes blurred with tears as she paid her fare to the driver.

Hearing the squeals and laughter of children, she walked around the redwood deck that surrounded the house. Alicia was leaning over the back rail calling down to the two boys chasing along the beach. "Adam, stop throwing sand or I'll make you come in."

"You wouldn't be that cruel, would you?"

"Sloan!" Alicia cried and rushed to embrace her friend. She clung to her, hugging her tight, making Sloan choke on her guilt. "God, it's good to see you. I'm so glad you came. Thank you."

"Don't thank me. I haven't done anything."

"You're here. That's a lot. Let's go inside."

"The boys—"

"They're forbidden to go near the water. It's too cold. I'll keep an eye on them."

"They're growing so fast," Sloan observed wistfully as she watched the two little bodies running gleefully in the sand.

"Yes, they are."

Alicia slid open a floor-to-ceiling glass door and led Sloan from the deck into Carter's house. The living room was tall and two storied. Suede sofas and chairs in beiges and browns were agreeably arranged around a brass fireplace. A fur rug of unrecognizable origin lay on the parquet floor in front of the hearth. Bright prints and colorful posters telling of Carter's travels around the world were hanging in brass frames on the white stucco walls. A spiral staircase led to a loft containing only a desk and chair. Its walls were lined with bookcases. The whole room was washed with sunlight. Sloan loved it. She was certain Carter had designed it.

"Lemonade?"

Alicia didn't wait for Sloan's answer as she went into the kitchen, separated from the living room only by an open bar. As she mixed pink frozen concentrate with club soda in a tall glass pitcher, Sloan let herself soak up the ambiance of the room. Carter's taste was impeccable. The reading matter in the cluttered bookshelves varied from philosophy and religion to erotica. His record collection was enviable. Seeing the things he surrounded himself with, Sloan felt as if she were touching his soul. She wanted to explore the rest of the house, but unless Alicia suggested it, she couldn't bring herself to ask.

"How was the flight?" Alicia asked as she handed Sloan a tall, iced glass.

"Noisy. There were two babies on board and neither was enjoying the trip."

Alicia made a valiant attempt to laugh. "Would you be too cold on the deck?"

"No. I'd like an unrestricted view of the ocean."

"You should have dressed more casually, but then you rarely do."

Sloan could have told her that last week she'd been tearing around San Francisco in jeans and sweaters under which she'd worn no underwear. But she doubted Alicia would ever believe it of her. Carter barely had, though that had been part of his prescribed therapy to "bring her out." "No pun intended," he'd said with a sly wink.

Today she was wearing a perfectly, if unexcitingly, tailored suit with a navy skirt and matching herringbone jacket. Her blouse was prim. Next to Alicia, in jeans and turtleneck sweater, Sloan felt stodgy. She wondered again how Carter could prefer her to her friend. Or had he only pretended to so she'd go to bed with him?

The thought almost gagged her. No. No. No. He might have left furious, proud, and insulting, but she couldn't—wouldn't—believe that his professions of love had been lies. She *wouldn't.*

Alicia stretched her shapely body onto a chaise. Sloan took a chair facing the ocean. The boys' laughter reached them. "I want you to see the boys later, but I want to talk first. Do you mind?" Alicia asked.

"Of course not. What's the matter?"

"God, you don't know how good it is to hear your sound, practical, steadfast voice." Alicia sighed and her full breasts quivered beneath her sweater. Sloan tried not to imagine Carter touching, kissing . . . "I'm so ashamed."

Alicia's wail brought Sloan out of her disturbing musings. "Alicia, please don't," she urged as wracking sobs shook Alicia's shoulders. "What's upset you? And what do you mean you're ashamed? I can't imagine you doing anything that shameful."

"Neither could I," she said, sniffing back her tears. "But I did. And it's that I don't regret doing it that's so shameful."

Sloan sat patiently, giving Alicia time to sort her thoughts. "I went to Tahoe that weekend after I came to San Francisco. I have a friend who has been divorced for several months and she's been after me to go out of town with her for a weekend. I swear to God, Sloan, I don't know why I went in the first place, except . . . Let's skip the reason for now. I went and I—I met someone. He was a good-looking man, nice, amusing, and we had a great time skiing together all day. And that night I—I stayed in his room and he made love to me all night and it was absolutely terrific."

She seemed vastly relieved that it was out. She shuddered on a long expulsion of breath. They remained silent for a long time. At last Alicia whipped her head around and faced Sloan with a degree of defiance. "Did I shock you speechless?"

Sloan shook her head before she could find enough voice to say, "No, no."

Alicia lay her head against the cushion of the chaise. "Of course I did. I shocked myself. I know you must think I'm a tramp, sleeping with a man I barely knew and liking it so much. How could you begin to understand, Sloan? A level-headed woman like you would never let herself go like that, throw caution to the wind, let the devil take tomorrow, do something she knew wasn't right."

Sloan's heart was thudding painfully and she felt like she might pass out if the thunder in her head grew any louder. She knew exactly what it was to sacrifice everything for passion's sake!

"I don't know what happened to me. Mountain

air? The only excuse I have is that I met Jim Russell when we were still so young. We married right out of college and had the boys within a few years. Then Jim was gone and I've felt so . . . old. Old and used up. Like life had passed me by before I'd even had time to enjoy it. Not that I regret my early marriage to Jim. I don't. But there's never been a time in my life when I didn't belong to someone else, when I was living solely for me." She looked down at the two children scuffling in the sand. "There will never be a time, will there?"

"Not if you marry Carter next week, no."

Alicia's bright eyes clouded with tears again. "That's why I feel so damn guilty about that weekend, Sloan. I love Carter, but . . ." Her voice trailed off and she plucked at a loose thread on her sweater. "Maybe I shouldn't confide this to you, but I've got to get it all off my chest. Carter and I have never, you know, been together. We've never gone beyond mild affection. Well, there was that one time at your house, remember when you came in my room and caught us kissing?" Mutely Sloan nodded. "You could have knocked me over with a feather! He's never been that way with me. And I . . . well, as passionate as it was, it did nothing for me. It's ridiculous, I know, but I felt like I was being unfaithful to Jim! Every time I look at Carter, I see Jim, and it's like we're cheating on him. I didn't feel that way with the man in Tahoe."

"Carter was Jim's best friend. It's natural that you'd feel that way," Sloan said for lack of anything better. A tiny beam of light was shining in the stygian darkness that had engulfed her since Carter left. She dared not hope that it could become a full-fledged ray of hope, still . . .

"In all truthfulness Carter's never . . . turned me on. He's just too good a friend. I guess after we're married I'll do what brides are expected to do. Even though he does nothing for me sexually, I have no doubt about Carter's virility. I doubt he'd tolerate a celibate marriage. We both want another child." Her voice trailed off into nothingness, its faint whisper carried by an uncaring ocean breeze.

Despite her inner turmoil, Alicia looked beautifully shy when she said, "Sloan, every time Mac— that was his name—touched me, I tingled all over. Do you know what I mean? Do you think I'm a terrible person?"

Sloan's soft smile was a trifle sad. "Yes, I know what you mean and no, I don't think you're at all terrible." With an affected nonchalance she asked, "This Mac, where does he live? Would you ever want to see him again?"

"He lives in Portland and he *said* he wanted to come see me. Of course I refused. I told him everything." She sighed deeply. "He's not really the point. The point is, I've limited my options." She sat up suddenly. "It's not that I want to be a bed-hopper. You know that, don't you?"

"Yes," Sloan said earnestly.

"I disdain that kind of life. I don't like my friend for living that way. She's probably had a score of men since the weekend in Tahoe and felt not one twinge of guilt. That's not me, Sloan. I could never cheapen myself that way, nor do that to the boys. It's just that I suddenly woke up to the fact that Jim might not be the only man I could love wholeheartedly and passionately.

"I thought that part of me was dead. It isn't. It's just been lying dormant and when Mac touched me, I was reminded that I am a woman, not just a widow and a mother and a close friend. I knew after my trip to San Francisco, after Carter kissed me that way, that he wasn't ever going to make me go weak-kneed. That's why I went to Tahoe in the first place."

"What will you do?" Sloan asked slowly. The light had become brighter and it was all she could do to sit calmly in her chair. She felt like shouting, like joining the children cavorting on the beach. Like an animal shedding its winter skin, she felt new and alive.

"I don't know," Alicia anguished. "Tell me what to do, Sloan." Pleading was in Alicia's crystal eyes and in her voice. "Tell me what a wonderful man Carter is. Tell me that with him there would be no risks. My sons and I will have security, safety. Tell me that their well-being has to come before my own selfish desires. Remind me how much Carter loves them and how disappointed and disillusioned he'd be if he found out that Jim's widow had slept with a stranger and loved every minute of it. Convince me that after we're married, when we're sharing a bed, that passion will bloom. Tell me all that, Sloan. Remind me what the decent, responsible thing to do is.

"Or," Alicia continued after a deep breath, "tell me to say to hell with what's right and to do what I want to do. If the truth were known, Carter might be relieved. He might only be marrying me because he feels an obligation to Jim to take care of us. Tell me to go to Carter and lay my cards on the table, to tell him I love him, but not in the way I should." Reaching across the space that separated them, she clutched Sloan's hands. "Sloan, for godsakes advise me."

"I can't," Sloan cried on a sudden burst of emotion. "Don't ask that of me, Alicia. I can't tell you what to do." If only she could. If only she could tell Alicia that it would be best for all concerned if she broke her engagement to Carter. One part of her was screaming, "Tell her, tell her. Make her decision easy for her. She'll be glad that you and Carter have fallen in love. Tell her."

It would take only one sentence. "I love Carter and I believe he loves me." She could tell Alicia honestly that they hadn't intended for it to happen, but it had. Now they could all have what they wanted. Sloan would have Carter. He'd have her. Alicia would be free to pursue her own happiness.

Another part of her was closing its ears to her heart's arguments. She couldn't interfere with Alicia's decision. Maybe Alicia loved Carter more than she realized. That weekend in Tahoe was the first time she'd been on a fling and she was still basking in the novelty of it. Her mind was remembering it more romantically then it had been. Later, she would realize that it was the steady, reliable kind of love that she and Carter shared that she needed.

No. Sloan could say nothing. If Alicia ever suffered any regrets because of this life-affecting decision, Sloan could never live with herself. She could never be happy with Carter if she had influenced Alicia to give him up. It had to be Alicia's decision, hers alone.

But please, God, let it be the one I pray for.

"Sloan, what am I going to do?" Lost in their thoughts, they stared at the two young boys playing on the beach. "They need a father," Alicia said quietly. "A father like Carter, but . . ." Again they fell silent, each running their separate gauntlet, fighting their way through their own hell.

Then David stopped his play and jerked his brother around, pointing toward the house. David yelled something and with the shorter, slower Adam in tow, began running toward the house, screaming at the top of his lungs.

Sloan and Alicia looked at each other in puzzlement. Then they heard David's lilting voice carrying across the wind. "Carter, Carter. Carter's back."

Turning simultaneously, they saw Carter just as he rounded the corner of the deck. When he saw Alicia's companion, he stopped with an abruptness as sure as if he'd walked into an invisible wall. The three were momentarily frozen in suspension while four sneakered feet tramped up the steps from the beach to the deck. Carter barely recovered from his shock at seeing Sloan in time to brace for the two small bodies launching themselves into his legs.

"You're back, you're back," David shouted, dancing a jig and clutching at Carter's trouser leg.

"Carter, will you buy us an ice cream cone? Mom said you could if we were good," Adam chimed in. "We've been good."

"Guess what. Our fish died. He's in Heaven with Daddy. But Mom said we could have another one."

"His stomach pooched out and he was floating on the top of the water. I saw him first and David didn't think he was dead, but I said he was."

Soulfully, Alicia looked into Sloan's eyes. Had she not been so wrapped up in her own misery, she would have seen her desolation mirrored in their smoky depths. A resigned smile tried to get a foothold on her lips, but didn't quite make it. "I really have no choice, do I?" she whispered for Sloan's ears alone.

Sloan shook her head, knowing that she had no choice but to remain forever silent, even if it killed her. "No."

"I knew that when it came right down to it, I wouldn't do anything else. I'll do what you would do. You'd do the right thing, Sloan. I know you would."

The *right* thing? Was damning three people to unhappiness the right thing to do? Yes. In this circumstance it was. Carter and Alicia would grow to love each other through the children who loved them both. Familiarity would fragment Jim's memory. They were both physically beautiful. Passions would flare when they realized that.

Yes. It wasn't ideal, but it was right.

Alicia gripped Sloan's hand one last time. Standing, she quickly turned and went into Carter's embrace. "Welcome home, stranger," she said cheerfully.

He enfolded her in an embrace made haphazard

by the two boys who still clung to his pants legs. Over Alicia's shoulder he looked at Sloan.

His eyes flashed a thousand messages and she received each one. He was sorry for the things he'd said. He had missed her. He was miserable. He was tired, weary of the world, of life without her. He was also asking what she was doing here at his house. He looked reproachfully at her clothes and the tight restrictions of her hairdo.

"I was lonesome for you, so I called Sloan to come down and spend the day with me," Alicia said, pulling him toward the group of patio chairs. Sloan's shoes could have been riveted to the spot, for she hadn't been able to move since seeing Carter. In spite of the fatigue pinching the corners of his eyes and mouth and the haggard blankness in his russet eyes, he looked marvelous. He had on a casual pair of slacks and a sport shirt with the sleeves of a sweater knotted around his neck.

"Hello, Sloan."

"Hello, Carter. How was New York?"

"Cold and rainy."

"You don't seem to be able to escape the rain," Alicia said, demonstrating amazing recuperative powers. "It rained almost the whole time you were in San Francisco, didn't it?"

"Yes," he said, his eyes melting into Sloan's.

"Boys, please stop pushing and come say hello to Sloan," Alicia instructed. Obediently they each mumbled a hello to Sloan.

She responded to their greeting with a smile that she hoped didn't look as brittle as it felt. "You've become fine young gentlemen since I saw you."

"Did you know my daddy?" Adam asked. "He died."

Sloan's eyes swept past Alicia and Carter who were standing arm in arm. "Y–yes I knew him. You're as handsome as he was."

"That's what Mom says. Carter's going to be my daddy now."

"That'll be wonderful, won't it?" Sloan didn't know how the words were surviving the crushing vise in her throat.

"Yeah, it'll be super," David contributed.

"Super, super, super," Adam sang.

"Go play now," Alicia said. "What about your book?" she asked of Carter when the boys had scampered to the edge of the deck. "Did you finish it?"

"Yes. It's already on the editor's desk. He said from what he could tell, it will be my best one."

"That's such good news, darling." Alicia squeezed his arm against her chest as she looked up at him eagerly. "You worked so hard on it."

"A lot of me went into this one." He tried not to look at Sloan, said to hell with it, and let his eyes gorge on the sight of her face.

"Does it have a happy ending?" Alicia asked.

Carter dragged his eyes from Sloan and looked down at his fiancée. At the moment her face was as innocent and guileless as her sons', and he felt like a bastard for the resentment he'd been harboring towards her. It wasn't her fault he'd fallen in love with the wrong woman. Raising bleak eyes back to Sloan, he answered solemnly, "It ended the only way it could."

As though his words had cut off her air supply, Sloan spun around frantically and rushed toward the door of the house. "I need to call a cab."

"No, Sloan, you must stay until after dinner," Alicia wailed.

"I can't. I have to get back."

"Stand right there," she said. "Don't do anything until I chase down David and Adam."

Alicia had been diverted by her sons' uncannily rapid disappearance, but not so Carter. He followed Sloan into the house. With an iron will, he had to lasso every muscle in his body to keep from going to her and taking her in his arms.

He cursed the dowdiness of her clothes, the return of the bun on the back of her neck, the guarded expression that masked the animation he knew her features capable of. That thin, tight-lipped mouth didn't even resemble the smiling, tempting one that had destroyed his senses with its loving generosity.

He longed to see again the passionate woman whom he knew lurked behind a wall of defeatism. Unimprisoned once, she could be freed again by his touch. But they were forbidden to each other by the dictates of their consciences.

Still, he couldn't let her go without her knowing how much he wanted her, how much he needed her, how much he loved her. He had to speak it aloud one last time or forever regret it. "Sloan, I—"

"Don't," she said through grinding teeth. Her back was to him as she braced rigid arms on the back of a chair. "Don't say anything."

"I've got to, goddammit."

"No. Please. If you do, I won't be able to stand it."

"Sloan, don't call a cab," Alicia said, stepping into the room, oblivious of the drama taking place. "The boys want to drive you to the airport so they can see the planes."

"No," Sloan objected quickly. "Carter just came from the airport."

"I don't mind."

"You stay, Carter," Alicia said. "I'll take Sloan now and you can pick her up next week when she comes for the wedding."

Sloan felt like Alicia had kicked her swiftly and firmly in the stomach. "I won't be at the wedding."

Now it was Alicia's turn to look dumbfounded. "But, Sloan, you have to be!"

Nothing on earth could compel her to sit and

listen to Carter pledging his love and life to another woman. Any woman. Even a woman Sloan loved, too. "I'm sorry, but I can't. I'll have guests at Fairchild House by then. I can't leave it. You'll have to consider the trip today my wedding congratulations."

Alicia looked upset and disconsolate. "But you missed my first wedding," she said petulantly. "I can't believe you'll miss this one, too."

"I hate to disappoint you, Alicia, but I can't . . . I can't be at your wedding."

Her tone brooked no arguments, though Alicia offered a few. Carter didn't say anything.

They left a few minutes later. Alicia was explaining to the boys how airplanes fly as she backed the car out the shell driveway.

Sloan risked one last look at the house. Carter was standing on the deck, staring directly at her. The wind was tearing through his hair. His hands were shoved into his pants pockets and his shoulders were hunched defensively, against the wind or against some internal enemy, she couldn't decide. His face, cast as it was in deep shadow, was inscrutable.

Which was just as well. Had Sloan seen the emotion shimmering in his eyes, she might not have been able to leave him no matter the consequences.

Chapter Ten

At least I still have this, Sloan thought as she served the custard with caramel sauce to the guests surrounding the dining table. Fairchild House was filled to capacity. All the bedrooms upstairs were occupied. Save one. But that one didn't count.

She would survive. She had before. She would again.

Fairchild House would require all her energy, physical and mental. This is what she was committed to. This was her life. Everything she had, she'd pour into making the bed and breakfast a success.

Friday evening. At two o'clock today Carter and Alicia had been married. He was permanently out of her life. From now on, her heart would belong to her business.

"It must have been dreadful. Wasn't it, Ms. Fairchild?"

She almost sloshed coffee onto her treasured Irish linen tablecloth. The conversation had flowed around her, but she hadn't been listening. She was startled to have a question directed to her.

"I'm sorry. What were you asking?"

"All the rain you had out here. It must have been dreadful." The woman was from the east coast and spoke with a nasal twang. She bullied her obsequious husband without letup.

Whenever the unseasonable weather that had made willing prisoners of her and Carter was mentioned, a misty look came into her eyes. "It was dreadful if one was required to go out of doors. More coffee, Mrs. Williams?"

Her voice was cordial and soft, unobtrusive, trained to give away none of her sadness. Only if one looked closely could he note the wistfulness in her eyes.

The guests filed into the parlor, four of them deciding on a game of cards. Sloan kept the coffee, liqueurs, and herbal tea flowing for as long as anyone wanted them. It was close to midnight before the last of the guests retired upstairs. Wearily Sloan went around checking locked doors and turning off lights.

She went into her room and crossed it in darkness, switching on a lamp on her bureau. Automatically she touched the lid of the locked lacquered box where it sat in a prominent place. A poignant smile played about the corners of her mouth and her eyes filled with eloquent tears.

It never occurred to her she wasn't alone.

Absently she reached up and drew the pins from her hair, one by one, slowly, until her hair fell in heavy waves onto her shoulders. She combed both hands through it, revolving her head on her neck to ease the tension of pretending happiness when actually grief as wide and deep as a chasm had severed her heart in two.

She unzipped her skirt and stepped out of it gracefully, folding it carefully over the back of a chair. The slip she was wearing clung to her hips, dipped and curved over the feminine delta, and detailed the shape of her thighs. Her hair fell forward and caressed wan, slightly sunken cheeks as she bent her head to better see the buttons on the deep cuffs of her blouse. Then the buttons tracking its pleated front were languidly released as she stared at some inspecific point in near space, lost in her thoughts. She was peeling the blouse off her shoulders when she happened to glance in the mirror and see him sitting in the easy chair across the room.

Her heart rocketed to her throat and stoppered a scream just before she could utter it. She spun around. The sudden action and the river of blood rushing to her head made her dizzy and blurred her vision. She grasped the edge of her bureau to keep from falling.

It *was* him, acting as though he sat in that chair every night and watched her perform this ritual. One ankle was propped on the opposite knee. He was holding a hardback book on his lap. His eyeglasses were perched precariously on the tip of his nose.

"Don't stop on my account," he said in a voice as seductive as his eyes which were touring her body with slow deliberation.

"What are you doing here?"

"Watching a most entertaining and stimulating striptease."

"Damn you, Carter, answer me."

All her frustration, heartache, despair roiled to the surface and she lashed out at him angrily. The torment wasn't over yet. Just when she'd become resigned to it, some malicious god had inflicted this dream on her. Or was this real? Was he really here, wearing that horrible fatigue jacket and looking much as he had the first night he'd arrived on her doorstep. "How did you get in? The doors were locked."

"Chapter five of *The Bishop's Kiss*." He held up

the book on his lap. "I was just rereading it now to see that I'd done it right. The point is moot, of course. I managed to break in the back door and relock it without anyone discovering me." His grin was boyishly proud. "I think I did it as well as Slater. He's the hero of this—"

"What are you doing here?" she fairly screamed, knotting her hands into fists at her sides.

Dropping the book and his eyeglasses on the floor, he lunged out of the chair and bounded toward her, plastering her against him with one arm and clamping the other hand over her mouth.

"You don't want to disturb your guests, do you, Ms. Fairchild?" he asked silkily, trailing his tongue down the side of her neck. "I didn't want to get rough, but this is what Slater did when he broke into the heroine's apartment. Not to mention our friend Gregory. We know to what ends he'll go to accomplish his goal."

She squirmed against him, trying to speak against his hand. "I can't understand you, Sloan. And you'd just as well save your breath and energy because you're going to need them." His mouth was at her ear now, moving in her hair, touching her lobe with the wet tip of his tongue. "You see I plan to make love to you all night or until we're both senseless, whichever comes first."

He captured her scream with the palm of his hand. "Did you say get out? Why? Oh, I know. You think I'm committing adultery. Wrong. I'm not married and I won't be until you can take a few hours off and we can run down to City Hall."

She sagged in surrender and became pliant against the rock hardness of his body. Over the heel of his hand, she blinked away furious tears and stared at him in wide-eyed incomprehension. "That's better. I hate to use force. But I wasn't sure I could stop you from screaming with this much more pleasant and much more subtle method."

Gradually he lowered his hand from her mouth and replaced it with his lips. He sealed them together with a sweet adhesion. She complied, at first because she was too bewildered to resist. Then the tongue that arrogantly caroused inside her mouth extinguished all thought except that she was once again in Carter's arms and he was loving her.

Her weak arms garnered enough strength to lift themselves to his shoulders. With greedy fingers, she plundered the hair that seemed perpetually too long on his collar. Her lips parted beneath his, flowering open for his tender violation. The magic lassitude that flowed through her veins like honey every time he touched her, afflicted her again. All her strength came from him, and suppliantly her body arched against the source of his energy in silent appeal.

"God, that feels good," he murmured as his lips ravished her throat. His hands cupped her bottom through the satin slip, lifted and pressed until he was snugly tucked into the shallow valley between her thighs.

"What happened?" she asked on a moan. "Why aren't you married? Don't hurt me again, Carter. Kill me if you must after you love me, but don't leave me again."

"Never. Never. I swear it. Can this go?" he asked of her blouse. She shrugged out of it as he pushed the sleeves down her arms. "I can see your nipples," he rasped in soft pleasure. "Don't you have on a bra?"

"I don't wear one anymore unless I have to."

"I love it, I love it." He fondled her through the cups of the slip. "But what made you decide that?"

"Because going without one reminded me of you. Kiss me there," she urged on a spiraling sigh as his fingertips found her nipple peaking with arousal.

He ducked his head and closed his mouth

around her, fabric and all. He wet the cloth thoroughly until it molded to and outlined her shape. "Look at you," he whispered reverently, his finger tracing the pouting point of her nipple. "I couldn't marry Alicia. I can't marry anyone but you, Sloan."

Her hands were busy divesting him of his jacket and shirt. When they were gone, her hands coasted over the fevered flesh and its crinkly blanket of dark hair. Sensuously her palms raked over his chest, back and forth until she was delirious with the variety of sensations. Her fingertips fanned across his nipples and they reacted suddenly and firmly. "Tell me what happened." Her tongue flirtatiously played with what her fingers had brought to distention.

"Sweet . . . Make them wet . . . Oh, God, yes, Sloan. I can't . . . can't talk when . . ." He fumbled with the fastener of his trousers. "Later . . . I'll tell you later. . . . Just know that I belong solely to you and that no one is going to be hurt by our being together."

"Carter," she breathed, repeating his name and loving the sound of it.

He hooked his thumbs under the straps of her slip and pulled it down over her love-swollen breasts. Her stomach rose and fell with agitated breath as he took the slip past it, then farther, taking her pantyhose as he went. When she was naked, his fingers sifted through the soft triangle of hair and caressed the slender thighs. His eyes swept over her like a prairie fire that crawls burningly over the plains. Taking her hand, he drew it to his pulsing desire. "Forgive me. I can't wait."

Sloan guided him to her own yielding moistness. "Nor can I." She trembled when he lifted her against him and carried her to the bed. He followed her down, shedding the rest of his clothes and kicking them free.

In one swift, sure thrust, he grafted her body to his. Exercising a tremendous amount of control, he framed her face with his palms and kissed her mouth with the same breathtaking intimacy of the other fusion. He delved deeply into its sweet wet warmth with his tongue.

"Feel how much I love you, Sloan Fairchild. From the first moment I saw you, I knew I had been incomplete until then. Know my love. Accept it. You are most worthy of it. It is I who humbly offer it. Sloan, make me whole."

Her body lay curled between his thighs, her legs and feet entwined with his. Her cheek was pressed into the hollow of his abdomen beneath his ribcage. Her hair draped him like a cloak woven of various shades of brown and gold. He threaded his fingers through it idly. Her fingers lazily circled the thick nest that housed his navel.

They lay replete after a crisis of volcanic proportions. Not once, but twice, exultantly free and guiltless passion had hurled them into another sphere. Now they were luxuriating in the sweetest exhaustion they'd ever known.

"Are you positive you're not just telling me that to make me feel better, Carter?"

"I promise. It was Alicia who asked to see me before the ceremony. We were at her parents' house. The wedding guests were already arriving. David and Adam had been spit-and-polished and were being guarded by the maid so they wouldn't get dirty. Alicia knocked on the bedroom door where I was getting dressed."

"You weren't dressed when you talked to her?"

He gathered a fistful of her hair and lifted her head. "Yes, I was dressed when I talked to her."

"Just checking," she said lightly, kissing the hair-dusted flesh with loving lips. "I'll have to keep close tabs on a husband who has a knack for breaking and entering."

"Yeah, I especially like the—"

"Entering," she finished for him. "You're shameless," she chided, twirling her finger in the well of his navel. "Proceed with the story."

"Alicia sat down on the bed and immediately burst into tears. She confessed what she saw as a dire transgression, making me feel like the biggest hypocrite in the world."

"You can imagine what I felt like when she confessed to me, saying that a woman like me would never do anything like that. And here I'd been sleeping with her fiancé. How did things ever become so complex?"

"We fell in love. No one, not even us, counted on that." He slipped his hand under her hair to massage her nape. "Then she started telling me what a wonderful father I'd make to her sons and how much Jim thought of me and how her parents thought I would be a marvelous provider. Your earlobes feel like the petals of a velvet flower."

The simple statement was so out of context that Sloan laughed. Carter drew in a sharp breath. "We're going to have another postponement of this story if you laugh again."

"Why?"

"Because I can feel the vibration of your breasts on a place that doesn't need any further encouragement to make me blissfully aroused . . . again."

"I'm sorry," she said without the least bit of contrition. Indeed, she let her hand drift farther down his torso. "I'm listening."

His breathing was jagged, but he continued doggedly. "I took both her hands and looked her straight in the eye and asked her if she loved me."

"To which she said?"

"To which she said yes."

Sloan levered herself up so she could look at him. The eyes which had been gleaming with devilish delight clouded over with turbulence. Carter ran his index finger along her lower lip consolingly. "She said yes she loved me, but not in 'that way.'

And when I asked her what way she meant, she said, 'Not in the way a wife is supposed to love her husband. Not enough to share your bed. Not enough to keep from wanting to return Mac's calls which I've been refusing.' Then to her great surprise, I hugged her and kissed her with more enthusiasm than I ever have, except for one time in this house that doesn't need to be recounted, and told her that I thought she was a perfectly wonderful woman for Jim and for some other fortunate man, but that I felt she might not be the woman for me."

Sloan had propped her chin on his sternum and was looking up into his face. "What did you tell the boys? Were they terribly disappointed?"

"Oh yes, they wept bitterly."

"Oh, Carter no!" Sloan said, ignoring his previous warning and jarring him with her shifting body.

"Oh, yes. They couldn't stand the thought of not getting to live at the beach."

Sloan's head dropped again to his chest as she slumped with relief. He chuckled and trailed a finger down the groove of her spine. "When they were assured that they could use the beach house whenever I wasn't there working, and when they were assured that I was still going to take them skating and to ball games and to get ice cream, and when they'd been served a piece of wedding cake, they were mollified."

"They do need a father."

He tensed as though to get up. "Well, if that's the way you feel, I can always go back to Alicia on my hands and knees—"

She spread her arms wide, closing her fingers around his biceps and holding him down on the bed. "They need a father, but not you."

"You're gonna keep me?"

She assessed him through narrowed eyes. "I'm

giving it careful consideration," she said after a long indecisive pause.

He closed his arms around her back and flipped her over, making their positions reversed. "Carefully consider this," he growled before he clamped his mouth over hers, his tongue plunging and dipping, circling and sampling, probing and persuading.

She panted beneath him when at last he scooted down her body and lay his head on the pillow of her breasts. "I'll certainly take that into consideration," she said breathlessly. For long moments they were still. She reveled in the feel of his hair clinging to her fingers, he to the steady drumming of her heart in his ear.

"Carter, did . . ." She wet her lips. "Did you tell Alicia about me?"

"Um-huh," he said with casual disinterest as he blew softly on a temptingly pink nipple.

Sloan knew a spasm of guilt and shame. "What did you tell her?"

"The truth," he said solemnly, raising himself up to peer steadily into her remorseful eyes. "That you were the hottest broad I'd ever laid."

"*What!?*" she cried, pushing him off her and sitting up. He collapsed onto his back, holding his stomach as he shook with laughter.

"You should have seen your face," he said, when his laughter finally subsided.

"Of all the horrible things to say," she huffed.

"Don't give me that, Ms. Fairchild." He yanked her down on top of him again. "Sell that prim and proper act to your customers, but not to me. I saw the real woman who was hiding behind that godawful robe you were wearing the night I got here. Tomorrow morning I'm going to personally see to it that that thing is burned." He hauled her up to his mouth and kissed her soundly while his hands smoothed over her bottom.

"In answer to your question," he said, when she

was once again lying along him in docile content-
ment, "I admitted to Alicia that you and I had
become very close friends and that I was returning to Fairchild House to see if my being engaged
to her had been the only deterrent to our becoming more involved."

"And was it?"

"Absolutely. I intend to become *very* involved."

She smiled against his chest. "And Alicia didn't
seem to care?"

He chuckled. "She may be more intuitive than
either of us give her credit for. She cocked her
head to one side and studied me shrewdly. Then
she said, 'There are a lot of bedrooms in that old
house and personally I think they could be put to
better use.' I took that as an endorsement. In any
event, she was laughing when I stripped off my
necktie and asked who was available to drive me
to the airport."

Sloan snuggled closer. "I'm glad," she said in a
whisper. "I couldn't have ever been completely
happy if *she* hadn't been the one to free *you*."

"Nor could I."

"What are we going to do?"

"Are you referring to the immediate future? If
so, that's a stupid question." His hand found her
breast and circled the dusky areola with a be-
witching finger.

"Um, yes," she sighed. "But I mean about your
house and your work and Fairchild House. I don't
want to give it up, Carter."

"You won't. I'd never ask you to, and I love this
old house. But, and I underline the but, there are
going to be some changes made. I'm bringing a
few bucks into this marriage and some of them
are going to be used to hire you some help. A
cook, someone to clean, someone to help you
serve—"

"But I love the cooking."

"And you can still do it. Just not all the time.

Some afternoons I may want you to be making wild love to me, not preparing bouillabaisse." He kissed her on the tip of her nose. "I could work here, even in this room. We can make this our base of operation, but I want you to take some time off periodically. I want to travel with you, take you places, show you things, show you off."

"Are you that proud of me?"

He could feel the tension, could sense the courage it took for her to ask that, and knew that only a few weeks before she wouldn't have had that kind of courage. She'd have reflected that defeatist attitude that she wasn't worthy of anyone's notice, that her existence was insignificant. His eyes lovingly touched each feature of her face, and in those amber eyes she found the self-confidence no one else had ever made her feel. "I'm that proud of you. You're the most lovable woman I've ever met. You always have been, Sloan. You just picked sorry candidates to show you how lovable you are."

"I believe that," she said, lightly touching his lips. "Because of you, I believe that. I am loved."

He pressed her palm to his mouth. "You are loved."

The emotion of the moment rendered them momentarily speechless. Finally he asked, "What did you think of my house on the beach?"

"I loved it," she said, her eyes sparkling. "It's beautiful."

"So it would be amenable to you if we lived there when we felt like it and lived here when we felt like and maybe hired a couple to run Fairchild House during our occasional absences?"

She pursed her lips in thought. "I'd be very particular about whom I left in charge, but I think I could live with that arrangement. It means a lot to me, Carter, to make a success of Fairchild House."

"You have," he whispered urgently. "And it certainly can't hurt its reputation to have a famous author in residence."

"A *humble* famous author."

"That goes without saying," he said seriously. Then his face broke into a broad grin as he settled her beside him once again. "Will you have a baby for me?"

"I'll have a baby for us," she said with quiet determination.

He murmured love words in her hair before asking, "What is in the box?"

"Box?"

"The one on your dresser. The one you came in and touched so reverently."

Slowly she disengaged herself from his embrace and walked naked across the room. Taking up the japanned box, she carried it back to the bed and silently extended it to him. He swung his legs to the floor and sat up, looking directly into her eyes as he took it from her.

He turned the tiny key with the black silk tassel dangling from it and lifted the lid. He knew at once what he was looking at without even reading the edited lines. He thumbed through the pages, before raising bewildered eyes.

"Why? You could have bought all my books if you didn't have them already."

The lock of dark hair that grazed his eyebrow was brushed back with an affectionate hand. "Anyone could buy your books. These discards were all I had left of you. No one else had ever read them nor ever would. They were exclusively mine."

"But, Sloan, they're the dregs, the trash. They're rotten."

She shook her head, fanning him with her hair. "How they read doesn't matter. To me they represent the most beautiful love story ever written. They are poetry."

In that way of his that she'd once found objectionable but now found endearing, he muttered what could have been a vile curse or a fervent prayer, depending on who heard it. She knew it to be the latter. He set her treasured collection of marred papers aside and wrapped his arms around her waist, laying his head on her chest.

"*You* are the poet. And the poetry," he whispered.

His hands skimmed her body, marveling over each texture, each swell and each hollow, the seeming frailty of her bones and the resilience of her skin.

His mouth rubbed against her breasts. "I need you, Sloan. I need your quiet encouragement, your intelligent insight on what I write. I need your understanding when it's not going well and your praise when it all falls together. I need the nurture of your sweet body."

A gentle push of his palm brought her nipple to his mouth and he kissed it with light fluttering kisses until she was aching with the love blossoming inside her. He took the delicate bud in his mouth and tugged on it with so sweet a yearning that her hands clenched in his hair and held his head fast.

"God, I love the way you feel inside my mouth, love to taste this." He lubricated her nipple with his tongue so it slid easily along his closed lips when he dragged his mouth across it with an erotic rhythm.

He loved her other breast just as ardently while his hands climbed the backs of her thighs from knee to hip. His fingers curled inward and upward when his mouth lowered to claim her navel. Hot kisses were rained on her and she was nuzzled by faintly whiskered cheeks. Her heart was frantic, her senses explosive.

Then his mouth grazed the golden down that veiled her femininity, and her spirit leaped to yet another level of splendor. Heeding the sweet request of his hands on the backs of her thighs, she tilted forward to receive his loving tribute.

Her fingers dug into the muscles of his back as she felt herself molding to the heat of his mouth, obeying the whims of his nimble tongue. Her body liquified in an attempt to quench his thirst.

But it could never be quenched. It was a raging thirst and one that compelled him to urge her down onto the bed and to sheathe himself in her love.

"Sloan, Sloan," he groaned in her ear as their bodies arched together. Calling her name, he experienced that small death that comes just before rebirth, and looking into her face he saw her own renaissance.

Later, when their hearts were pulsing together more sedately, he gathered her to him. "You'll coach me through writing the great American novel, won't you?"

"I'd be honored."

"You'll put up with my black moods?"

"I'll love you out of them." His hand cherished her breast without passion, but with a great deal of loving gratitude. "Will you begin right away?"

"I have two things to do first."

"What?"

"Have a honeymoon at Fairchild House."

She covered his hand and pressed it tighter against the globe of her breast. "What's the other?"

"To change the last few pages of *Sleeping Mistress*. It's going to have a happy ending."

THE EDITOR'S CORNER

For all of us who work on the LOVESWEPT series this should be one of the happiest holiday seasons ever! Our joyous spirits are directly attributable to our marvelous authors who've been turning in their most splendid work for us to publish for you. I can't think of anything that's more fun than playing Ms. Claus, helping to deliver these gifts of truly entertaining, truly moving love stories.

Laura London and Robin James are two of my favorite authors . . . and yours, too, I'll bet. And guess what? Both Laura and Robin are really the happily married couple, Sharon and Tom Curtis! Next month you'll read their first (but not their last!) LOVESWEPT, #25, **LIGHTNING THAT LINGERS.** Sharon's and Tom's love story of the tender, yet worldly Philip Brooks and the soft-hearted, yet hardly worldly Jennifer Hamilton is so original and written in such a magical style that I'm sure it will affect you deeply. The hero's occupation is unique in category romance publishing, the heroine's shy charm and wit are a delight, as are two winsome little owlets and an outrageous "hunk" named Darrell. It is hard to characterize this creative contribution to the genre and I do not wish to give one surprise away. So, I will only comment that all of us on the LOVESWEPT staff feel that **LIGHTNING THAT LINGERS** is a breathtakingly memorable romance.

The letters you've sent us about Billie Green's two previous LOVESWEPT romances have been heartwarming—and so expressive of our own reactions to her writing. "I have never laughed so hard or felt such emotion from a book before," wrote one woman about Billie's first LOVESWEPT. Others comment, too, on

(continued)

her humor, her gentle and yet steamily sensuous way with a love story. A reader even sent a note thanking Billie's mother for passing on that delicious "tetched" quality! In LOVESWEPT #26, **ONCE IN A BLUE MOON,** you can look forward to another simply delightful story from Billie. I believe this book has one of the most original, exciting—and, yes, humorous— love scenes that it has ever been my pleasure to read! Arlie, the heroine, has been Dan Webster's cross to bear since the day they met when she was a wild child and he a teenager. She suddenly reappears in his life and wants something very special from him . . . a very *personal* favor that will certainly surprise you as much as it surprises Dan! An absolutely delicious romance ensues, full of scrapes and sensuousness and heart rending emotion.

Here in the office we have wonderful battles—good-natured, but hard-fought—over which of Iris Johansen's heros is the most delectable. At the moment Nick O'Brien, whom you glimpsed in this past month's **THE RELUCTANT LARK,** is winning. And he's the hero of **THE BRONZED HAWK,** LOVESWEPT #27! (I adore Iris's use of characters from one book to the next, don't you?) Nick—that highflyer with women, that irresistibly handsome genius—is about to get his wings clipped! The young lady who grounds him is a feisty, golden-haired reporter named Kelly. Iris was so emotionally wrung out by creating **THE RELUCTANT LARK** that she said she just had to reverse gears and create a romp in this work. Indeed **THE BRONZED HAWK** is wonderful fun! It demonstrates so beautifully what a versatile talent is our own Iris Johansen!

There's an "insider" story about this book that I can't resist sharing with you. We take great care in checking the accuracy of factual background in our LOVESWEPT romances to back up our authors. A crucial piece of **THE BRONZED HAWK,** but amounting to only a few paragraphs in the action, involved Nick and Kelly bailing out of a hot air balloon using just one parachute. Our editor had the time of her life double checking this one! The result was that a high placed officer of the Eastern Airborne Division of the Army provided expert authentication and even had his class of cadets run through the scene several times to make absolutely certain the procedure was correct! You'd be amazed at some of the lengths to which we go— and get others to go along with us—to check even minor references in our LOVESWEPT romances!

Two more pieces of fabulous news to brighten the holiday season. Anne Reisser's last book was published in September 1982, and I know you have been anxiously awaiting her next one. Well, it's a LOVE-SWEPT! **LOVE, CATCH A WILD BIRD**, #28, will be out in January 1984. And Kay Hooper (also known as Kay Robbins) has also become a LOVESWEPT author. Her romance, **C.J.'S FATE**, LOVESWEPT #32, will be published in February 1984.

We send you our warmest good wishes for a happy holiday.

Carolyn Nichols

Carolyn Nichols
  Editor
LOVESWEPT
Bantam Books, Inc.
666 Fifth Avenue
New York, NY 10103

Love Stories you'll never forget
by authors you'll always remember

THE LATEST BOOKS IN THE BANTAM BESTSELLING TRADITION

☐	23800	**MISTRAL'S DAUGHTER** Judith Krantz	$4.50
☐	14200	**PRINCESS DAISY** Judith Krantz	$3.95
☐	14628	**WHITE TRASH** George McNeill	$3.50
☐	01487	**MORNING STAR** Kerry Newcomb (A Large Format Book)	$6.95
☐	20823	**DIFFERENT FAMILIES** Alison Scott Skelton	$3.50
☐	23291	**JERICHO** Anthony Costello	$3.95
☐	23105	**NO COMEBACKS** Frederick Forsyth	$3.95
☐	22749	**THREE WOMEN AT THE WATER'S EDGE** Nancy Thayer	$3.50
☐	23028	**WINDBORN** Victor Brooke	$3.50
☐	23026	**CAPRICE** Sara Hylton	$2.95
☐	22924	**PUBLIC SMILES, PRIVATE TEARS** Helen Van Slyke w/J. Edwards	$3.95
☐	23554	**NO LOVE LOST** Helen Van Slyke	$3.95
☐	23071	**A RAGE TO LOVE** Liz Martin	$2.95
☐	22846	**THE DISINHERITED** Clayton Matthews	$3.50
☐	22838	**TRADITIONS** Alan Ebert w/Janice Rotchstein	$3.95
☐	01415	**FLAMES OF GLORY** Patricia Matthews	$6.95
☐	22751	**A PRESENCE IN A EMPTY ROOM** Velda Johnston	$2.50
☐	22577	**EMPIRE** Patricia Matthews w/Clayton Matthews	$3.50
☐	20901	**TRADE WIND** M. M. Kaye	$3.95
☐	20833	**A WOMAN OF TWO CONTINENTS** Pixie Burger	$3.50
☐	20026	**COME POUR THE WINE** Cynthia Freeman	$3.95

Prices and availability subject to change without notice.

Buy them at your local bookstore or use this handy coupon for ordering:

Bantam Books, Inc., Dept. FBS, 414 East Golf Road, Des Plaines, Ill. 60016

Please send me the books I have checked above. I am enclosing $_____ (please add $1.25 to cover postage and handling). Send check or money order —no cash or C.O.D.'s please.

Mr/Mrs/Miss_____

Address_____

City_____State/Zip_____

FBS—11/83

Please allow four to six weeks for delivery. This offer expires 5/84.

DON'T MISS
THESE CURRENT
Bantam Bestsellers

☐	23637	**THE THIRD WORLD WAR: THE UNTOLD STORY** Gen. Sir John Hackett	$3.95
☐	23481	**THE VALLEY OF HORSES** Jean M. Auel	$3.95
☐	22775	**CLAN OF THE CAVE BEAR** Jean M. Auel	$3.95
☐	23670	**WHAT ABOUT THE BABY?** Clare McNally	$2.95
☐	23302	**WORLDLY GOODS** Michael Korda	$3.95
☐	23353	**MADONNA RED** James Carroll	$3.95
☐	23105	**NO COMEBACKS** F. Forsyth	$3.95
☐	23291	**JERICHO** A. Costello	$3.95
☐	23187	**THE TOMBSTONE CIPHER** Ib Melchoir	$3.50
☐	22929	**SCORPION EAST** J. Morgulas	$3.50
☐	22926	**ROCKABYE** Laird Koenig	$3.25
☐	22913	**HARLEQUIN** Morris West	$3.50
☐	22838	**TRADITIONS** Alan Ebert w/ Janice Rotchstein	$3.95
☐	22866	**PACIFIC VORTEX** Clive Cussler	$3.95
☐	22520	**GHOST LIGHT** Clare McNally	$2.95
☐	22656	**NO TIME FOR TEARS** Cynthia Freeman	$3.95
☐	23224	**A SEPARATE PEACE** John Knowles	$2.50
☐	20822	**THE GLITTER DOME** Joseph Wambaugh	$3.95
☐	20924	**THE PEOPLE'S ALMANAC 3** Wallechinsky & Wallace	$4.50
☐	20662	**THE CLOWNS OF GOD** Morris West	$3.95
☐	20181	**CHALLENGE (Spirit of America!) #1** Charles Whited	$3.50
☐	22615	**DESTINY #2** Charles Whited	$3.50
☐	23106	**POWER #3** Charles Whited	$3.50

Prices and availability subject to change without notice.

Buy them at your local bookstore or use this handy coupon for ordering:

Bantam Books, Inc., Dept. FB, 414 East Golf Road, Des Plaines, Ill. 60016

Please send me the books I have checked above. I am enclosing $_____
(please add $1.25 to cover postage and handling). Send check or money order
—no cash or C.O.D.'s please.

Mr/Mrs/Miss_____

Address_____

City_____ State/Zip_____

FB—11/83

Please allow four to six weeks for delivery. This offer expires 5/84.